THE LAST CELTIC WITCH

The Last Celtic Witch

Lyn Armstrong

Resplendence Publishing, LLC
http://www.resplendencepublishing.com

Resplendence Publishing, LLC
P.O. Box 992
Edgewater, Florida, 32132
Copyright © 2007, Lyn Armstrong

Warning: All rights reserved. The unauthorized reproduction or distribution of this copyrighted work is illegal. Criminal copyright infringement, including infringement without monetary gain, is investigated by the FBI and is punishable by up to 5 years in federal prison and a fine of $250,000.

Original trade paperback printing October, 2007
Second trade paperback printing March 2008

This is a work of fiction. Names, characters, places, and occurrences are a product of the author's imagination. Any resemblance to actual persons, living or dead, places, or occurrences, is purely coincidental.

DEDICATION

I would like to dedicate this book to my daughter, Alyssa, whose generous spirit and beauty inspired the heroine in this book.
I love you Kitty Kat

ACKNOWLEDGEMENTS

Many thanks go to my critique partners, (The Writing Girls) and Florida Romance Writers, Inc for their unyielding support and belief in me. And a special thanks for Leigh Collette and Jessica Berry of Resplendence Publishing for allowing me to shine like a star. Much love to my Moon Sisters

CHAPTER ONE

Scotland, Highlands

"Please, not again," Adela MacAye softly pleaded. On her knees, she leaned against the edge of the lumpy bed, her hands clasped tightly before a miniature statue of Amerissis, the Goddess of Light. "I beg of you, please give me a different vision."

She rose gingerly from the hard dirt floor, tied her brown hair into a taut braid, and flipped it over her shoulder.

"I know not why I keep praying, Amerissis. My visions never change."

She wiped her moist, slim hands on her gray kirtle and collapsed onto the cushions of a worn, red velvet chair stuffed with feathers.

Looking around her modest cottage, she sighed with resignation, her shoulders slumped. How did she find herself to be in such a remote, barren land far away from her mother's rose garden in England?

"Fear," she scoffed aloud. Fear had caused her to spend most of her life running. Once the town folk suspected the plain lass on the edge of the village to be a witch, she was forced to leave each provisional home or be burned at the stake.

Adela shivered, recalling her mother's gruesome death. She was of only twelve winters when a vicious mob dragged Mary MacAye out of their home. Accusing her mother of communicating with the devil, they burned her alive in the middle of the village.

It mattered not that Mary, sweet in nature as she was beautiful in face, helped villagers over the years with their ailments. People still feared her mother, showing revulsion toward her when passing on the road.

Foreseeing her mother's death was not a vision Adela wished for, but it had given them enough warning to be prepared when the angry villagers battered down their door. Mary had pushed Adela out the back window with supplies and coin before the villagers could capture her as well. Adela begged her mother to run with her, but she smiled and said, "You cannot escape fate." Mary kissed Adela's tear-stained face, and firmly pushed her daughter away.

Adela had hidden in the thick forest and followed from a distance as they dragged her mother away and tied her to a stake around which firewood was piled. Tears blinded Adela's vision, but she knew there was nothing she could do but watch the flames climb higher. Her mother's screams echoed in her ears while the smell of burning flesh caused her to vomit the meager contents of her stomach.

After the screams died, the villagers went back to search for the little witch, but she had vanished. Adela knew of the safe path that led her away from England, with all its ignorance and prejudice against her kind.

Perspiration beaded on Adela's upper lip. She leaned back in the chair and closed her eyes. Like the day when she had foreseen her mother's death, she now had visions of the tortuous events leading up to her own demise.

Perhaps after ten winters her vision would be different and her fate changed.

Slowly her breathing became centered and calm, her

muscles relaxed. She went through the ritual of visualizing a white light around her body while asking Amerissis for the gift of sight.

Gently, her spirit eased from her body and traveled up through the thatched roof of her run-down cottage. Her body remained still on the chair, yet Adela could see everything from above, separate yet connected by a silver thread that joined her spirit to her body. Weightless and free, she flew through the cloudless sky.

Forest animals near the lake glanced up at her as she drifted by. In body they would be afraid of her, but in spirit form they accepted her presence as peaceful and loving. She waved at the creatures and sent from her heart a light that would give them protection from predators and mankind.

Adela looked beyond to the home of a young Scottish clan. The parents were busy washing clothes and cutting wood while their children played on the edge of the woods, happy and carefree. Adela shifted her gaze, wishing she had the love and simplicity their lives afforded.

Swiftly her spirit pulled toward the nightmare she knew was coming. Gliding over the darkened mountains and into an eerie mist, she was guided to a place of great sorrow and pain.

No! Please, not again.

The large familiar castle hunkered on the mountainside; its surrounding battlements towered over small buildings within. The castle itself stood bold and intimidating to all who looked upon its black stones.

Her vision remained the same, and so too, her fate.

Before she could scream, her spirit reappeared inside the castle's dungeons. Dark and damp, she floated above the putrid rushes on the stone floor and saw her future self being thrown into the dungeon by grim soldiers. The darkness overwhelmed her senses, yet she heard the pitter-patter of rats scattering across the filthy rushes. She saw herself sobbing, rocking back and forth, chanting, "I will not be afraid. I will not be afraid."

She heard noises outside and her focus shifted from her weeping body to the small, barred window. In the bailey below, a stake awaited her with a mounting pile of firewood. Adela moved closer to her future body and reached out to touch her shaking shoulder. The door swung open with a bang and they both looked up.

Unwilling to watch the soldiers drag her future self away to be burned; Adela's spirit retreated from the dungeons and their impenetrable walls.

Her spirit flew through the sky and she swiftly arrived back at her safe cottage, where she joined with her present body once again.

Adela's eyelashes flew open, every muscle in her body shook with fear and apprehension.

Soon she would be imprisoned and sentenced to death.

She could try to run, leave in the night. But her visions were never wrong. If she was meant to die, she would die, no matter how far or how fast she ran.

But to die a maiden, never having known a man's touch or to give birth to a child and pass on the MacAye blood, a sacred witch's blood that would end with her death…the thought was unbearable. Resisting the urge to collapse in tears, Adela shot to her feet, her hands fisted at her sides.

"I will have a baby! And my legacy will pass on to another generation. Even if I am not around to watch my child grow, I will honor the past MacAye women. Our line will not end with me."

She lifted her chin and swallowed the knot lodged in her throat, her tone even. "I will not fail you, Mother."

Blowing a stray hair away from her face, Adela rushed to the cupboard. She banged the timber doors open and shoved the cupboard's meager contents into a coarse bag. It did not amount to much, but the bread and mead would prevent her from starving. Her wooden chest scraped along the ground as she pulled it out from beneath her bed. Opening the lid, she rummaged through the clothes and changed into an old travel gown of blue-green.

Running her fingers through the braid, she loosened the knot and flicked her hair loose down her back. Adela grabbed a cream cloak from the wooden hook by the door, threw it around her shoulders and raised the hood over her head, covering her features.

Determination settled like a rock inside her stomach. "There is not much time, but there is still a chance!" she reassured herself, rubbing her neck.

Opening the old creaky door, Adela stepped boldly into the morning light. She took a deep breath and forced a high-pitched whistle through her two front teeth.

From out of the woods a white horse materialized, its mane and tale flowing in the wind. The majestic beast galloped toward her, its hooves sliding on the dewy grass before it halted in front of her.

"Greetings, my old friend," she said. "I have need of your sight."

The mystical creature tossed his head and the comforting smell of horse-pelt filled the air.

Adela raised her voice, "I call upon my heart's desire. Show me a man who will sire. I need someone gentle, it is my first time, someone who is pleasing and will not ... will not ..."

Adela struggled to find the ending to her spell.

A giggle escaped her lips and a sparkle entered her eyes. "I call upon my heart's desire. Show me a man who will sire. I need someone gentle, it is my first time, someone who is pleasing and will not whine."

A rose-pink orb gathered in her hand, and she placed

the energy over the horse's forehead. "Take me to this man."

The horse nodded his head and scraped a hoof in the dirt. Adela kissed his soft velvet nose. She grabbed a handful of white mane and vaulted onto his back. "I am ready to find the father of my child."

* * *

Muted autumn sunrays scattered across the sky, gently caressing the distant rolling hills. Yet the scenic beauty was lost on Sir Phillip Roberts. The stench of death surrounded his every step on the battlefield. His jaw ticked as he surveyed the damage. The skirmish against Lady Torella's army of Campbells had been particularly brutal. Much blood was and still would be spilled for the ownership of Phillip's ancestral lands. His eyes narrowed when he walked over another wasted, lifeless body and cursed under his breath. "Only a lad, this one was," he said. Lifting his head, he called to the remaining soldiers, "Here's another one."

Three men rushed over to prepare the corpse for transport back to their hidden camp. "We must make haste before the sun sets. These woods will be crawling with Campbell scouts once they regain their strength."

"This is the last one," a young squire informed him.

"Take him with you and I will follow once I find my horse."

Phillip's anxious chestnut stallion waited near the edge of the woods. The beast snorted with fear, his brown eyes wide. He too was eager to be gone from the valley of death.

Phillip swung into his saddle and had picked up the reins when from the corner of his eye he saw a white streak run through the trees. He squinted. There it was again ... a woman in a flowing white cloak danced carefree through the trees.

Was she daft? This was no place for a lady to be

frolicking in the forest. Enemy soldiers and mercenaries would penetrate these woods once they had the cover of darkness.

"Har!" Phillip spurred his horse toward the fleeting vision. She had to be warned.

But where could she have come from? There was nary a cottage or village for many leagues. Unquestionably the noises of a recent battle would discourage a hapless traveler from entering these woods. Had she not heard the din?

Once within hailing distance, Phillip stopped his horse. "My fair mistress, this is no place—"

Her cloak fell to her shoulders, allowing him a glimpse of silky brown hair that fell in gentle waves down her back. She stopped dancing and became deathly still as if she had turned into a statue. His eyes traveled down her backside to two bare ankles peeking from beneath an unadorned green dress. She glanced over her shoulder and giggled, then darted away like a deer.

Phillip chased after the woman, his mount dodging trees and fallen logs, following brief glimpses of her gown. How could she continue to out-maneuver his agile warhorse?

Halting his mount in an open meadow, he scanned the area for the mysterious lass, but she was nowhere in sight. A feminine hum floated on the breeze and he jerked his head around to follow the sound. A sweet melody came from a small pond barely hidden by tall grass.

Dismounting, he led his horse closer to the grassy wall. The humming stopped, but sounds of splashing mingled with the clop of his horse's hooves. Phillip cleared his throat loudly, alerting the lass to his presence. "I wish not to frighten you, but 'tis not safe in these woods for you to be unescorted."

The urge to peek through the green cover to see if the lass swam naked was almost too much to resist. He heard a swishing movement in the water and then a rustling of grass. Phillip stepped back, eager to finally see the face of the mysterious woman.

Her lilting voice echoed through the swaying, green wall, "But clearly ... I am not alone."

The grass parted and a woman of no more than twenty-five winters stepped into the clearing. Dripping, russet hair framed high cheekbones and an adorably upturned nose sprinkled with freckles. Her gold-flecked eyes spoke of innocence, yet also glistened with tentative seduction, as if the lass were eager to explore pleasures not yet known to her.

Phillip's gaze was drawn to the emerald gown plastered to her wet skin and the outline of her pert breasts, their erect peaks pressed tightly against the damp material.

Immediately his manhood stirred beneath his kilt, his heart rate increasing. She had the appearance of an enchanting nymph.

"Do you like what you see?" she asked, her face flushing deeply.

"I ... well ..." Phillip was torn between devouring the maiden with his eyes and averting his lust-filled stare as any honorable knight should do.

Finally he turned his back on the tempting nymph and ran his hand distractedly through his wavy hair. "This is no place for you to linger, Mistress ..."

"My name is Adela of the MacAye clan." She sighed with frustration. By Jupiter! Why did she have to pick a respectable male to father her child? And one so incredibly handsome that he made her feel more homely than ever.

Biting her lip, she stepped closer to his form, a study in languid power. Masculine smells of wood and horse floated from his lustrous hair, which skimmed the wide set of his shoulders. It was a stark contrast to his dirty and bloody kilt. He was obviously one of the soldiers who had battled on the field yonder.

Strange that the bloodstains did not repulse her, but merely increased her attraction to the imposing figure. Her gaze dropped to the strong hands clenched at his sides. She imagined him wielding a deadly, heavy claymore, his full lips firm with determination. A ripple of pleasure swept over her skin.

Could those same brutal hands caress my body with gentleness?

Adela touched his shoulder and he pivoted, knocking her backward. He reached out to catch her before she fell and held her in his arms. Dear Goddess, he was the most attractive man she had ever seen. Even with an angular jaw, high arched eyebrows and a wicked scar across his cheek, he was as beautiful as an angel sent from heaven, and looked as if he would be more at home in a church than with a sword in his hands.

And his eyes!

The soldier's gaze reached out to Adela, affirming his desire for her, and something else ... a vague loneliness?

Using her powers, she created a voice inside his head. "*Make love to me. I am willing.*"

The beguiling words echoed in Phillip's mind, urging him to do as she bid. She felt so fragile, her slim hips pressed against him. He should release her. It was improper for him to keep holding her, yet he could not get his muscles to obey. She felt so right in his embrace. Bending down, he picked her up and carried her through the grass to the nearby pond.

Cradling her in his arms he lay her down on the soft grass, his lips close to hers. Her breath smelled of sweet raspberries mixed with mild spices. It made him smile, picturing this nymph picking berries while dancing through the woods.

Perchance, this is the afterlife and my body is actually lying dead on the battlefield?

If that be the case, then he would indeed make love to the nymph. If it was to be the last thing he did, why resist this divine creature in his arms?

Lowering his lips, he hesitated for only a moment before capturing her generous mouth with hungry urgency.

CHAPTER TWO

Adela opened her lips, allowing his tongue to dance with hers in lingering exploration. Her heartbeat pounded in her ears and her head swam with his taste and nearness while she absorbed the sensual energy of his masculine essence into her very core. He moaned deep in his throat and Adela arched her body closer to his, her hands caressing the back of his head.

She pulled slightly away, forcing air into her burning lungs. "I ..." She glanced down at his damp tunic where it touched her wet gown. "I have wet your tunic."

Shrugging, he hovered above her mouth and murmured, "Then we best take off our soiled clothes before we catch the death."

Adela nodded slowly, mesmerized by his intense sky-blue eyes and the pressure of his lean body against hers.

"May I have the honor of undressing you?" he asked, his voice a deep rumble.

"Aye." Her stomach churned with nervous anticipation.

His fingers deftly untied the laces from neck to waist, exposing skin with a scarlet flush of arousal. Gently, he peeled the wet fabric away from her sensitive, pink-tipped breasts.

The warm breath of his lust-filled sigh swept over her

breasts and Adela clenched her fists, unsure of what to do with her hands when the rest of her body thrummed with such intense sexual energy. Her chest rose and fell with each laborious breath as she yearned for him to touch her. He kissed two fingers and then circled them around the outside of her aching breasts. As a cat would antagonize a mouse, his eyes were alight with a devious glow.

Adela arched her back, eager for her taunted nipples to be caressed. Why did he not fully touch her breasts? Was he driving her insane for a reason?

Staring into his eyes, she bit her lip with wanting, silently pleading for him to end her torture.

"Do you want me to touch them?" he asked, his voice low with desire.

"Please," she whispered.

Finally, he cupped both of them, warming them to his touch. A gasp escaped Adela's lips, a surge of pleasure filled her womanhood.

His eyes widened with surprise at her passionate reaction. "Is this your first time, lass?"

"Aye."

"Are you sure you want to continue?" His tender hands kneaded and stroked her breasts.

She wanted to scream, *"By Jupiter, soldier! Of course I do. Your hands are driving me to the brink of madness."* But instead she answered, "Aye, I want it more than anything."

"As you wish," he said and lowered his lips to suckle a nipple.

Lifting her head, Adela watched his tongue swirl around her protruding, velvet tip. She squeezed her thighs together, the ache between her legs increasing with every flick of his tongue.

Lowering his other hand, he gathered the folds of her skirt and ran his fingertips up her legs, the pressure firm and possessive against her skin.

When the gown reached her waist, he pulled away from her breasts to find she wore no undergarments. His gaze caught on the thatch of dark brown, curly hair nestled between her thighs. The primitive gleam of a warrior entered his eyes, and she matched the hard intent of his stare with one of her own.

Rising her arms, she allowed him to lift her gown over her head, his movements becoming urgent. Adela rested back on the grass and watched his torso muscles tighten when he hastily pulled the woolen tunic over his head. Blond hair blew with the breeze while he twisted to throw the garment with careless abandonment.

His magnificent body belonged in heaven, not here on earth with mere mortals. She could not believe he found her attractive, although, the look in his smoldering eyes said he did. Adela had never felt so beautiful, so worshiped.

Lying beside her, he reclaimed her mouth, his kiss fierce and passionate. The back of his fingertips ran down the side of her abdomen, tracing a heated trail upon her skin.

"Spread your legs further apart," he whispered against her lips.

She obeyed without hesitation, the craving unbearable within her slick, warm flesh. Adela knew she should be shy and modest, yet being naked in front of this man felt so right.

So natural.

He eased his fingers between her moist folds and rubbed her sensitive core with the pad of his thumb. She moaned against his lips and his tongue plowed into her mouth, smothering her gasps of rising pleasure.

Her body tensed and she entwined her fingers through his hair, holding his head fast to their savage kiss. Tremors of rapture spread through her body and spirit as she bucked beneath the onslaught of his expert fingers.

Before her breathing could settle, the soldier swiftly rose, leaving her feeling bereft of his sensual energies. Her gaze followed his every move. He twisted out of his kilt and discarded it, leaving his swollen shaft thrusting outward, masculine and potent.

Adela had spied on the village men when bathing; their soft members intrigued her maiden curiosity; however she had never seen one rigid or quite so impressive before. She tensed, wondering if he would fit inside her.

Sensing her discomfort, he lay down on his back, beside her, and lifted his arms behind his head. "My sweet lass, you may have full control. Pleasure yourself upon me and I pledge to you, I will make no demands you are not willing to give."

Adela's eyes widened. "Do you speak false words?" Hungrily, her gaze roamed every inch of his muscular form, only to rest again on his straining erection.

"Nae. You are welcome to test me."

Swallowing hard, Adela sat upright and tentatively touched his warm chest. The light sprinkling of hair was soft beneath her hand. A sweet light scent of perspiration and leather filled her senses, arousing her again.

Her hand ran over every ripple of muscle leading toward the coarse hair surrounding his manhood. Unsure of herself, she glanced at his handsome face, his lust-filled gaze encouraging her to touch his sleek hardness.

Biting her lip, she entwined both hands around the base of his shaft and lightly ran them up to the satin tip and back down again. Her chest tightened with excitement and she shyly peeked at the soldier to see if he, too, felt the tension. His eyes were closed, his head back on his hands. A groan sounded from his lips and she continued the motion with rhythmic pressure.

"Do you like this?" she asked, knowing the answer,

but wanting to hear his rich, timbered voice.

"Aye, you are doing well, lass. Keep it steady," he answered, the veins on his neck standing out.

He groaned again, and jerked his head to the side in wild response. Adela smiled with wicked satisfaction that she could tease as well as the handsome soldier. All of a sudden he gripped her hand tightly, stopping the movement.

A sheen of sweat broke upon his forehead. "If you wish not for me to spill my seed in your lovely hands, you'd best stop now."

Smiling seductively, she threw her leg over his waist, straddling the throbbing flesh beneath her. "I would not waste your seed so carelessly."

"Vixen." Taking a deep, fortifying breath, he continued. "Take me at your leisure. For you, I will slay any who dare intrude on our paradise."

Nodding, her eyes bore into his and she gradually lowered herself onto his staff. Bit by bit, she tenderly pushed him further into her wet sheath until her maidenhead was broken.

Adela's eyes squinted with uneasiness, her insides burning, stretched to their limits.

Without pulling out, he sat up and cupped her face. "Give yourself time to adjust to my size. I pledge the pain will ease." He kissed her on the lips, tender and slow.

Adela rolled her hips from side to side, and instead of feeling pain, she felt stirrings of pleasure. "You were right, soldier. This does feel good."

He groaned with suppressed frustration, his head fell back to the grass. Another smile of triumph crossed her face and she continued to wiggle upon his erection. She fell over his body, her brown hair caressing either side of his face. Adela kissed him again and rocked back and forth, tipping her hips.

He strained beneath her, and Adela rode him with wild abandonment, eager to consume more ecstasy, feeding off his groans of passion. She never wanted this euphoric sensation to end. Her hips thrust faster and faster while her heavy breathing mingled with his. She arched backward and screamed her release as he did the same, spilling his hot life force into her with an explosive shudder.

She stared at him in amazement and they both laughed with the incredible impact of their lovemaking. She fell beside him on the grass, his arm cushioning her head. His fingers affectionately caressed the side of her shoulder. The simple caress gave Adela a warm feeling in her stomach. So this was what intimacy felt like. She liked it.

Her hand lightly brushed across his chest, and she casually threw her leg over his leg. She should ask his name, but in a way did not want to know.

It was best if the name of my baby's father was unknown.

That way he would remain a fantasy in her mind forever. Not real, yet human enough to sire a child. She almost wished there could be a future for them, but once he found out she was a witch, he would be repulsed like all the other men before him.

"What are you thinking?" His eyes searched hers.

Unwilling to spoil the moment with her thoughts, Adela's gaze caught on the wicked scar along the side of his cheek. "How did you get that?" she asked and trailed her finger along the smooth indent.

"If I tell you, you will believe I am daft."

"Think you I do not already?" she said with a mischievous twinkle in her eye.

Phillip's deep chuckle vibrated through Adela, deliciously prickling her skin.

He brought her palm to his lips and kissed it. After a long pause, he finally answered, "I took a blade to my face and marked my skin."

Adela gasped. "Why? Why destroy something so beautiful?"

Somber, Phillip leaned back and placed his free hand behind his head. "We live in a world where brutality and strength is all that matters to a man. So, a boy with an angelic face, I was taunted mercilessly. And not only by the other lads, but by my father who was disappointed that his son favored his mother's fair looks."

Adela's eyes softened and her voice lowered, "And you thought they would respect you more if you had a scar?"

"Aye."

"Did it?"

"Nae. My father gave me a thrashing. Said if anyone was to be scarring me it would be him." Phillip rolled over and propped up on his elbow, facing Adela. "I think he felt remorse for his role in my foolish plan and did not know how to apologize."

"From that day forward, he did not taunt me about my looks or allow the others to do so in his presence. But I did have to prove I was not a weakling to everyone and to myself." He picked up a strand of her hair and smelled it with appreciation, then continued. "I practiced relentlessly with a claymore and became more determined in training than most boys. When it came time for challenging battles, it was soon apparent my fair looks did not interfere with the skill of my sword."

"For which clan do you soldier?" Adela asked absently, her gaze resting on his captivating lips. How could any maiden resist such a man? And he was all hers for this moment in time.

"Roberts's clan, however, I am not one of the—"

Unable to wait any longer, she kissed the exceptionally beautiful warrior. Savoring the taste of his mouth, she deepened the kiss with her tongue. Adela knew she should be listening to what he was saying, but his lips were mesmerizing and she craved to reclaim his mouth. God's wounds, his sculptured torso felt so good against her breasts.

A piercing caw echoed overhead and Adela jerked in his embrace. "Did you hear that?" she asked, terror lacing her words.

"What?"

"Over there." She pointed to the sky. "'Tis a raven!" she whispered, her body tensing.

Fear, stark and vivid, sliced through her.

"Why dread the black bird? 'Tis harmless," he said, his brows furrowing with concern.

The raven flew over them again, his sharp call vibrating though her soul, sending shivers of foreboding down her body. "Evil is watching us." She firmly grasped his arm, her nails digging into his flesh.

"Phillip!" several male voices called from a distance. "Phillip, where are you?"

Another male yelled, "Come hither. There be his horse."

Phillip turned to the girl in his arms. "My men are searching for me." Releasing her, he rose and stood at the edge of the pond, his nakedness covered by the tall grass. "I am over here, but do not enter. We will come out."

Phillip turned around to find that Adela had vanished. "Lass, all is well. You will not be harmed," he called across the pond, but she did not emerge from hiding.

His bare feet splashed through the edge of the pond as he rushed over to the other side and searched for her in the grass. He could not find her in the thick overgrowth.

"Don't you think this is an inappropriate time to bathe?" Dougal said. The heavily built War Trainer stifled a chuckle as the rest of his men gawked at Phillip bent over in the brush, his naked buttocks exposed.

Phillip straightened, unconcerned with his men's whispered jests. "There was a woman ..."

Dougal nodded, rubbing his red beard. "Right, lad. I think you have had too much sun. Best you get back to camp and take a nap."

"Do not patronize me. There really was a ..." At the disbelief in his men's eyes, he finished, "never mind. She would be impossible to catch now. Let us away."

Shrugging into his clothes, he passed Dougal and playfully pushed the hefty man's shoulder. "You big oafs scared her off."

"Sure we did," Dougal retorted.

Mounting his horse, Phillip surveyed the area once more for any sign of the enchanting creature with which he'd had the honor of passing the afternoon.

"Come on Phillip," Dougal said. "The men grow restless and wish to find their ale and a bed."

"Aye," Phillip offered, and rode back through the trees, cursing his forgetfulness to ask the lass from where she hailed. MacAye, MacAye. He had never heard of the clan before.

* * *

Within the dark forest, Adela calmly waited next to her horse, comforted by the shadows hiding her form. It was not as if she loathed sunlight, but was accustomed to walking through the woods under the soft moonlight, her solace undisturbed by curious people who wished to pry into her life.

The white horse nudged her shoulder and she leaned her cheek against his solid, warm neck. The musky scent of her friend filled her with companionship, nevertheless, she sighed with loneliness. "You know I need to let him go," she murmured, her chest tightening.

The distant sound of a horse's neigh sounded through

the towering pines. Adela's head lifted and she edged around a black tree trunk, her hand caressing its rough bark as she strained to see through the thick forest. The soldiers were finally leaving the meadow and returning through the woods, but Adela's gaze was trapped by only one of them. The most commanding in stature and desirable of them all.

She glanced down at her stomach and placed a loving hand over her abdomen. Returning her stare to his retreating back, she breathed wistfully, "Farewell, soldier known as Phillip … and thank you for our babe."

* * *

A silent raven perched above, hidden within the thick branches. Black, beady eyes glared with menace at the woman swinging onto a horse. A metallic scent filled the air, and the raven lifted his beak. He opened his wings for flight.

His mistress had beckoned him.

CHAPTER THREE

Seven moons later, Phillip dismounted from his warhorse and gave the reins to his squire. He swore beneath his breath and rubbed the aching muscles of his sword arm. The bloody feud lasting more than three years against his family had him in a foul disposition. He has had enough of this senseless war.

Careful not to slip in the sludge, Phillip strode down the hillside through the camp. He glanced at his soiled tunic and kilt. Again, he was covered in blood and dirt, his black boots perpetually scuffed with mud. Perhaps it was not the endless battle that had him vexed, but the futile search for Adela that had him frustrated. It was as though the lass were a spirit of the nether world. Here one moment, vanished the next.

Three tired soldiers stumbled across Phillip's path and he stepped aside, allowing them to pass. On the morrow they, too, would be on the field once more, fighting the persistent Campbells.

Phillip sighed with relief when his tent came into view. He could not wait to wash off the blood and collapse on his bed.

"Sir Phillip, your grandfather requests your presence," a man-at-arms announced behind him.

Suppressing a moan, Phillip glanced down at his

stained hands. "I will clean up first," he responded and turned his back.

"I beg for your pardon, but the laird cannot wait."

Phillip turned and nodded with resolution. "Lead on."

He entered the tent his grandfather occupied, scattered with sparse luxuries. In war, the Roberts Chieftain did not live in comfort when his men were dying on the fields.

Phillip walked over to his grandfather, who lay ill in bed, his ashen cheeks sunken and his gray eyes dull. Even at the age of sixty winters, the old chieftain remained handsome. An ancestral trait of the Roberts clan.

The old man's eyes brightened when Phillip entered.

"My boy, you are safe."

Phillip sat on the chair beside the makeshift bed. "Aye, Grandfather. The Campbells are hearty soldiers, but they have no passion in the fight."

"In sooth, I have no passion to be fighting them," the old man croaked, "but one must stand against the devious Lady Torella. The merciless reiving of our lands, the killing of our people and livestock has to be stopped."

"Aye, I had hoped her father's death would alleviate her need for more land, but alas, her greed has not sated."

The old man coughed, his slender body wracked with spasms. He pushed himself upright in bed, his weakened lungs splattered blood on the coarse blankets.

Phillip twisted around to retrieve a jug from the table beside him, and poured water into a chalice.

"Grandfather, is there naught I can do for you?" he asked, handing him the goblet.

"Nae." He drank heartily and winced as if the cool liquid scorched his raw throat. "Curse this feeble body that steals my strength."

"You must not overtax yourself."

The chieftain grabbed his grandson's arm and looked solemnly into his eyes. "You must pledge to me an oath before I die."

"Grandfather—"

"Pledge!"

"What be the oath, my laird?"

"Pledge you will do whatever you must to bring peace to our clan."

Sighing, Phillip nodded with an assurance he did not feel. "I swear to you, Grandfather. It will be done." He rose from the chair and walked to the entrance. "Now get some rest. I must go back to the battlefield. The men—"

A wheezing sound came from his grandfather, and Phillip turned to find the chieftain's blue eyes were glazed. His chest no longer rose and fell with breath.

Returning to the bedside, Phillip took his grandfather's rough sword hand and fell onto the chair.

Inside, he felt empty, numb. He rubbed his dry eyes and sighed. His grandfather was the last of his family. Leaning over, he rested his forehead on the edge of the bed. He had not the luxury of grief. He was now chieftain of the west Highlands, a powerful laird. Yet he did not feel it. His deceased father was a legendary warrior, as was his grandfather. Both had ruled with fairness, wisdom and strength.

How could he live up to such a legacy?

Phillip pushed to his feet and raised his chin. He must not let his people down.

He glanced once more at the body of his last remaining relative. "I will not disappoint you, Grandfather. Peace will reign in our land. No matter what it takes!"

* * *

Weary from making arrangements for his grandfather to be sent home for burial, Phillip exited his makeshift home and joined his men-at-arms at the fire. Talk of the day's battle and their conquests had them arguing about who had killed the most.

"I swear to you, I have killed twenty Campbells on this day," Richard, a short burly soldier with a wart on his bare chin, announced.

"Hah, twenty-eight Campbells felt the point of my blade," a lanky man boasted.

"You must jest, Seamus. E'eryone knows you cannot count that high," teased his twin brother, Thomas.

Phillip winced at their blood thirst on the eve of their chieftain's death.

"Have you no shame?" Phillip's voice rose. "Your leader is barely cold and you crow over victories."

The soldiers looked at their feet and mumbled their apologies.

Phillip pivoted and stormed away, only to be followed by Dougal, whose hefty build, red hair, and thick beard added to his fierce appearance. Dougal had only to growl at a soldier to have him fainting with fright.

Although the same height as his friend, Phillip's skill had won him many practice fights with the elder, battle-hardened soldier.

"Think you I was harsh with the men?" Phillip asked, slowing for the trainer to join him.

"Aye. You know they risk their lives for the clan. When the day's battle is complete and they still live, they must find courage in their prowess of steel to last another day on the bloody field."

"Aye," Phillip answered with regret, his body slumping with exhaustion.

They walked in companionable silence to the river that weaved alongside their camp. The peaceful currents moved before him as he stared into their depths, wondering how the river still flowed with certainty of its direction when death polluted its waters.

Phillip kneeled. Cupping cold water in his hands, he scrubbed the blood from his skin. He wished he could just as easily erase death from his heart.

He was the last of the Roberts and now felt truly alone.

Dougal crouched beside him. His gaze was heavy on Phillip. "What are your orders?"

"I do not know," Phillip answered. "I must have peace amongst our clans. Still, Lady Torella will not be reasoned with. I dare say she will spill the blood of every man in the Highlands before giving up the prospect of taking our lands."

"May I offer a suggestion, my laird?"

"Have out with it, man."

"Why not give it to her?"

Phillip stared at him. "Have you been knocked on the head too many times, my friend?"

Laughing, Dougal shook his head. "Marry the lady, join lands and call an end to this feud."

"Are you daft? Lady Torella hates all Roberts. She would never marry me."

"A man of your comely looks can seduce any woman," Dougal said, winking. "A woman has never said nae to you."

"Even so, Lady Torella would by no means agree." Phillip added with sarcasm, "It would take an enchantment to have her thaw to me."

"Exactly."

"Pardon?"

"A love potion," Dougal said, a single eyebrow arched.

"A love potion?" Phillip laughed. "Now I *know* you have been hit on the head."

"I know of a witch who can make you a potion that will have the beautiful Lady Torella begging to be yours."

"I do not believe in witches," Phillip said, his tone firm.

"'Tis worth a try, my laird. They say she is ugly to

look upon, but has the magical touch of the fey."

"I am surprised a warrior such as you believes in superstition."

"Do you wish to have peace?"

"Aye, but—"

"Then have the witch summoned and see for yourself, my laird."

"Verily well, then. Have her brought to Gleich Castle. And I will see for myself if these rumors be true." Phillip went to leave, and then turned. "Have the men return home to their families on the morrow. There has been enough death on both sides."

Bowing, Dougal replied, "As you command."

CHAPTER FOUR

The thud of muddy boots rang on the stone floor as Dougal marched through the great hall of Carline Castle. Servants scurried out of the large Highlander's way, his barbaric reputation and murderous scowl produced fear in all who stumbled across his path.

He grasped his claymore, and it glided silently out of the scabbard. With a determined stride, he reached the mistress's chamber and pushed open the heavy oak door.

His eyes adjusted to the darkened interior while feminine moans of pleasure filled his ears. Upon the large bed sat the beautiful and naked, Lady Torella. Her smooth lily-white backside moved up and down, straddling a male slave. Her thick, black hair swayed with each thrust of her hips. Watching Lady Torella's exposed, heart-shaped buttocks, Dougal pursed his lips, enjoying the sweet view of her tight hole.

She needed to be speared and speared hard.

Torella's musky scent surrounded him and he breathed deeply. His shaft ached for the inner caverns of her loins. He threw down his sword, and it clattered on the stone floor. In a swift motion, he undid his chausses and stood behind Torella. Leaning over her, he grabbed her ample breasts and guided his straining erection up her arse while she moved in rhythm to the servant beneath her.

Unwilling to share her, Dougal lifted her up and threw her face down on the bed, her plump buttocks still embracing his shaft. He growled at the incensed slave, and the young man's face paled and he scrambled off the bed.

"Harder, Dougal," Torella moaned.

He seized her hips and thrust deep. The clinking of his chain mail mingled with a tight-jawed growl.

Her muscles squeezed from inside, and a throbbing heat shot up his groin. He had plundered many a wench in the backside but none gave the same stimulation as Torella. Concentrating on not losing his load before she reached her peak, his body glistened with sweat. Od's bodkin, she felt incredible!

Stay the pace, stay the pace!

Finally, she screamed her release, pushing her slippery buttocks harder against him. She was insatiable and Dougal was only too eager to pump his seed into her. Just when he was about to yield to his physical need, she rolled away, left him unfulfilled and aching for more.

Twisting around, Torella kneeled on the bed before him, her breasts pressed against his chain mail. She lightly kissed his lips, teasing him. Rolling her pink tongue along her mouth, he knew she took glory in the sexual pain she caused.

"Will he seek the witch?"

"Aye," Dougal breathed, the veins in his forearms standing out. "He promised his grandfather he would bring peace to the clan before the old man died from the potion you gave me."

He clenched and unclenched his fist at his side, his manhood standing boldly erect. The need for satisfaction was excruciating. But he knew her game and must play by her rules or be left unsatisfied.

"Excellent. This pleases me well."

Torella grabbed hold of his swollen flesh and rubbed

from the base all the way to the tip. Her hand increased in speed while her wicked smile stretched with victory at her prowess.

With his hands on his hips, Dougal threw his head back and groaned, his body rigid and ready for an explosive release.

Torella's eyes shadowed with malevolence and she halted the movement of her skillful hands. "Beg me!"

Tight lipped, he remained silent.

"Beg me or leave."

"Pl...please," he said. "Keep going."

Her jade eyes glittered with triumph and he scowled, hating the power she held over him.

Torella worked her practiced hand until he bellowed with release. His warm ejaculation shot over her flat abdomen and curly ebony hairs nestled at the apex of her thighs.

She lay down on the soft ruby coverlet, her hands resting behind her head.

"Now lick your seed off me. Then lick my ... sheath ... clean."

Lowering to his knees, the most feared soldier in all the land obeyed with unrelenting abandonment.

* * *

Adela had failed. She had failed to become pregnant by the soldier in the woods, and the vision of her death remained the same. Time was running out!

The MacAye powers would end with her life and all good magic would vanish from earth. How could her spell have led her to the wrong man? How could Phillip not be the chosen one?

She swallowed the defeat in her throat and hastily rose from her chair to make ready a sack of herbs and potions. If she was going to be captured, she might as well be prepared. One could not cheat fate after all. Did not her mother die with those same words on her lips?

In the early morning light, her nervous fingers fumbled with the small black leather sack she would hide in her kirtle. Soon, very soon she would be taken away. A crackle of energy snapped in the air close to her shoulder. She jumped and turned, searching for the source.

A sharp caw echoed from the kitchen window, and Adela jerked her head to find a black bird sitting on the ledge.

"A raven!"

Shutting her eyelids tight, Adela envisioned a white protection light swirling around her body. She tentatively opened an eyelid, her heartbeat hammering in her ears.

"Get out of here!" she shrieked, waving her hands about wildly.

But the raven returned her look with contempt, its beady black eyes glaring at her with arrogance.

"Leave!" she yelled, her voice stronger with fortitude. Adela picked up a bag of sage and threw it at the intruder. The bag landed pathetically short, and the raven mocked her with another eerie cry.

Its long black wings stretched wide and it flew off the ledge, but not before leaving Adela with the notion her future was doomed.

A chill ran down her spine with a vision of horses thundering through the woods, the soldiers' expressions grim with their determination to find to her.

"They are coming," she said aloud, and gathered her meager belongings before opening the front door.

Calmly, she closed the door behind her, and faced the direction the soldiers would appear out of the thick, dark forest.

Ironic, that with death approaching she could be somewhat composed. She would face her fate like her mother had done. With pride and dignity. She did not regret being a witch, nor would she apologize for her powerful lineage.

The heavy thud of horses' hooves pounded on the forest floor. Adela tilted her head up to the sun. This would be the last time she felt its warmth. With a deep breath she closed her eyes and allowed the balmy rays of the Celtic Sun Goddess, Grian to surround her body, filling her with courage.

Several soldiers erupted from the dark forest; their banners marked with the black wolf crest of the Roberts clan. The chieftain's men abruptly halted before her and dismounted.

A handsome brawny soldier with a beardless face and wild, blond hair stepped forward with authority. "Are you the witch who lives in the woods?"

"Would there be any other?"

The soldier looked confused and shared a glance with one of the men behind him.

Adela sighed. "Aye, I am the one you seek."

"Know you we were coming?" the soldier asked bewildered.

"Aye, I knew," she answered, and allowed the soldier to lift her up onto a bay mare. Without looking, Adela could feel the soldiers ogling her. Their fear and disapproval weighed heavily on her as they rode side by side. She was used to the stares of people who knew not of the gentle powers she wielded. Their ignorance made them afraid, and their fear had killed her mother and would have her condemned on this day.

A strong urge overcame her to kick the horse into motion and try to outride the soldiers, but she suppressed it. She would not be able to outride her fate, no matter how fast the horse.

The somber group rode for most of the day in silence until they reached Gleich Castle. The imposing edifice perched on the side of the mountain, appearing as though it were carved out of the a towering cliff.

With the setting sun behind the mountain, muted shadows cast over the raised village within the impassable fortress walls.

It must be nice for the occupants within to sleep safely at night, Adela mused, knowing the battlements would keep enemy raiders out. If only she could cast a spell to have them sleep while she escaped. Adela shook her head, dispelling the thought. It would take more power than even she possessed.

Large wooden gates creaked open, allowing them to pass under an iron portcullis before entering the lower ward. Their horses' hooves clopped over the cobblestones through the village toward the imposing castle. Small cottages with colorful flowers on their windowsills lined both sides of the path, contrasting with the gloomy wall that stood behind them.

People came out of their homes to gape at her. Adela guessed they did not know she was a witch. Otherwise she would be peeling their rotten vegetables off her clothes. At least she could be grateful for the chieftain's discretion.

Perhaps he planned to use her flaming execution as a surprise amusement for his people. Despite her bravado, she shivered with apprehension. She did not want to die.

* * *

With a chalice of red wine in hand, Torella glided over to the stone pillar holding a metallic scrying bowl adorned with emerald stones and Celtic symbols of ancient sorcerers. Carefully, she poured in the dark liquid and it swirled continuously, a grey light illuminating the contents.

"Show me what I want to see," Torella intoned, resting her long nails on the edges of the enchanted bowl.

An image appeared of the MacAye lass riding into the bailey of Gleich Castle. The witch's fear was so delicious;

Torella could almost taste it. Dipping her finger into the wine, the picture rippled. She licked the tart liquid from her fingertip and laughed. Soon she would have the witch's power. She had waited ten long winters to restore her ageless beauty and youth.

Torella walked over to the large glass mirror with iron candle sconces along the edges. Sweeping her hand across the tight skin of her face, she searched for any signs of aging.

Enchanting the Campbell chieftain into believing she was his lost daughter was easy enough. The power of commanding the chieftain's virile soldiers gave her a delightful diversion while searching for the MacAye witch. But she soon grew vexed with her father's interference.

'Tis a shame he suddenly became ill and died a painful death, leaving me with everything.

"He was a fool," Torella said to her stunning reflection, and lifted her chin up to inspect the skin beneath.

Her eyes widened with shock. A wrinkle! Edging closer to the mirror, Torella squinted at the faint line under her chin.

If she did not take the witch's power by the full moon of Samhain, all would see she was a three hundred year old sorceress. She must have the girl's powers!

Rushing back to the scrying bowl, she glared at the image of the witch being taken into the castle by two soldiers.

"Aye, take her. Take the virtuous witch to meet her true love."

CHAPTER FIVE

With a soldier on either side, Adela was led into the great hall to stand in front of a high, empty chair. The soldiers promptly left and she scanned the deserted chamber. Different clan shields, swords, and rich tapestries adorned the walls, giving the room a warrior appeal.

Crackling sounds came from a fireplace behind the high table. Adela shuffled to the side and shifted from foot to foot, becoming hypnotized by orange flames hungrily consuming the dry timber. She swallowed the nervous lump in her throat, and diverted her gaze.

The smell of cooked meat wafted in her direction, and she inhaled the delicious aroma of beef, lamb and chicken. Against the walls stood trestles filled with food of every description, including garden vegetables, exotic fruits, and pies of various sizes and shapes. Adela's mouth watered and her stomach rumbled, her eyes widening as they gazed upon each delectable platter.

"Stealing food from the chieftain's table is a decision not wise," Adela admonished herself, her tone holding less than conviction. Scanning the empty hall again, she wound a finger in her hair. "What can they do to me? Burn me at the stake?" she added with a crooked smile of defiance.

Her blue skirt rustled around her bare feet, brushing over the clean rushes. Unsure what to eat first, she picked up a chicken leg and ripped into the tender meat. Its savory juices ran down her chin, but she was so hungry she did not care. She took another bite when masculine voices drifted inside the hall and the herb-flavored chicken lodged itself in her throat. Bending over, she coughed, her eyes watering.

Straightening, she swallowed the lump and breathed deeply. Her mouth still watered from the tangy herbs and she glanced with longing at the poultry in her hands. Would she have enough time to chew one more bite?

Throwing caution away, she ripped into the delectable flesh one more time. Chewing faster, she rubbed her chin and shoved the chicken leg into the front pocket of her kirtle. Covering her mouth, she ran back to the spot where she had originally been delivered and stood deathly still.

The door behind her opened with a bang and Adela jumped, but did not look. The sounds of boisterous men echoed off the walls while soldiers filed into the great hall and sat down. Adela did not look at anyone, but kept her eyes downcast and her hands clasped behind her back, still rapidly chewing the food in her mouth. Why did she take such a big bite? Curse her appetite!

The soldiers did not pay much attention to her, and for the first time in her life she was happy to be homely. Beyond being curious about why she stood in the middle of the hall, they ignored her to satisfy their own hunger.

Adela had almost swallowed the last of the meat when a large man with flaming hair and beard circled her. Adela stopped chewing and avoided eye contact.

"Is this the witch?" he bellowed behind her.

"Aye," the blond soldier answered from his table.

"What be your name?" the man asked, his tone intimidating.

"You are scaring the lass, Dougal." A familiar rich, timbered voice echoed through the hall.

With one last gulp, Adela swallowed and looked up at the man about to sit in the chieftain's high chair.

Her lips parted with surprise as she stared blankly at the angelically handsome man garbed in black. That was no laird sitting before her. It was Phillip, an ordinary soldier who had taken her maidenhead. Heat flooded her cheeks when he appeared to recognize her.

Adela swallowed again, but this time from nervousness. How could he be the Highland laird? His dungeons were in her vision and his bailey would hold the stake that would see her burned to death. Had fate thrown them together for a reason?

She ached all over as if an invisible hand plunged through her chest and squeezed her heart. What was this feeling? Adela looked down at her clammy hands and wiped them on her kirtle. Suddenly her mouth went dry and she looked back at the chieftain, her heart thumping. Could this be the man she was meant to be with? Not only the father of her child, but the love she had waited for all her life?

"She smells!" Dougal accused.

Adela frowned and edged away from the strange man.

"Chicken! I smell chicken!" he announced, as if expecting applause. When blank stares from everyone were his only response, he added, "She has been eating chicken."

"Dougal..." said the chieftain.

Dougal grabbed Adela's hand and checked her pockets. Finding the lump, he pulled out the chicken bone and held it high in the air. "She is not only a witch but a thief!"

"I ... I ..." Adela wondered how she was going to explain herself.

"The lass is obviously hungry. Give the food back to her and sit down!"

Shoving the meat back in her kirtle, Dougal turned and

went to sit by the chieftain.

"Not here, Dougal. Find another seat for the eve's meal."

With the chieftain's displeasure evident in the slash of his eyebrows, everyone in the hall watched the furious trainer pivot and walk away.

Phillip's intense blue gaze settled on Adela. "I have searched e'erywhere for you. Please, come sit by me and let us eat."

Adela blinked rapidly, her mind in a haze with mixed emotions. One moment she prepared herself to be thrown into the dark dungeons to await her death. In the next she stood in front of the bonny soldier with whom she had once been intimate. Nae, not a soldier. A chieftain who held her life in his hands.

"If you prefer, you may dine in the village," he offered.

"Nae, nae. I am content to dine with you," she said, and slowly walked to the high table. The closer she got to the chieftain the more her hands shook.

He rose and pulled out the chair for her to sit, and Adela smiled at him. His height and muscled body were as she remembered. Tall and powerful.

The usual peaceful energy surrounding her suddenly turned erratic as if she were being charged with a lightning bolt. Adela took a deep breath, trying to calm herself and settled into the seat beside the man who knew every inch of her body.

"Adela, where did you go?" he asked, serving her a trencher of food. "But first, tell me from where you hail, so I do not lose you again."

Her attention went to the morsel he dished, watching the way his long fingers picked up a piece of bread and added it to her plate. "I ... I come from the MacAye clan."

The chieftain smiled at her stuttering. Adela guessed

he was used to women making fools of themselves over him. She frowned, wishing she had the same confidence she had at the pond.

"Your accent is slightly English, but you have a Scottish name?"

"Aye, I am traveled, and my mother was Scottish. I never knew my father."

"Where is your mother now?"

"She is dead," Adela answered, her eyes lowering.

"Are there no others in your clan?"

"Nae."

He covered her hand. "So, you are alone?"

"Aye."

"Then allow me to introduce myself. I am—"

"Laird Phillip Roberts, Highland Chieftain. I know who you are. You are the last of the Roberts clan. If you do not marry and produce an heir, your lands will be considered easy for the taking."

"Aye, you have the right of it." He shifted closer to her, his eyes holding a dubious look. "So you are a ... witch?"

"Aye, I am a ... witch," she said in the same tone as the laird's.

"I see," he said and looked away.

"Do you?" she replied, an edge to her voice. "If you had known I was a witch, you would never had made love to me, is that the way of it?"

"Nae, I mean, aye. I do not know."

Although she was not surprised, her heart ached from his answer. "Well, let us start with something you do know. Why did you bring me here if not to prosecute me for being a witch?"

The chieftain shifted on his seat to face her. "I do not believe in witches, but I am in dire need of help. Therefore I find myself opening my mind to any possibility."

Adela nodded, finding a small measure of respect for someone willing to learn about what others scorned. "Please go on."

"I would like you to make me a love potion so Lady Torella will accept my offer of betrothal and end this senseless feuding," Phillip replied, curious why his heart raced with uncertainty, as if her opinion of him mattered on this subject.

His gaze roamed over her brown hair pulled back into a tight braid. One he wanted desperately to undo and run his fingers through. He closed his eyes tightly then opened them. Images of her innocent, naked body opened up to pleasure as he plundered her warm, slick—

"Are you listening?" Creases etched around Adela's warm honey eyes.

"I pray your pardon?"

"It would also give you extra land, strengthening your position as laird," she said, her tone even.

"Aye, it would, but that is not the reason why I want the potion," Phillip replied. He paused to draw a breath and shifted on the chair to ease the snug fit of his swollen staff. Resisting the urge to explain himself to her, he gruffly asked, "Will you help me?"

"Nae."

"Nae?"

Nodding she turned away and started to eat. Phillip studied her profile. Although most would say Adela was plain in face, he found her looks enticing. A pert freckled nose gave her cheeks a sweet appeal as did her finely sculpted lips. But it was her golden-brown eyes that spoke of an awakened passion only he had discovered. His heart swelled with possessiveness. If only he could offer her a hand fasting. Living with the spirited Adela would certainly be a life free from tedium. Shaking his head free of foolish daydreams, he cleared his throat. He must remain focused on duty.

"Is it that you ... you can not make a love potion or that you *will* not make a love potion?" he asked, irritated he was now the one stuttering.

Lifting a piece of bread to her soft pink lips, she sighed and replaced it on her trencher. "To every potion or spell that is cast, there is an opposite effect which occurs elsewhere in the world."

"I do not understand," Phillip confessed.

"The world is in balance and Fate uses her divine power to keep it that way. If I were to cast a fortune spell, I would be temporarily wealthy with a grand castle like yours, but one day a warlord might burn it to the ground. Then I would be left with exactly what I had before I cast the spell, thus making the world balanced."

Phillip frowned. "So, if you were to make me a love spell, my betrothed would end up hating me?"

"Aye, or she could fall in love with another while being married to you. The spells do not always work out the way they were planned. There have varied consequences. If your fate was to love a ... another ... then you would love another, yet Lady Torella would still be in love with you."

Phillip looked into her eyes, his brow furrowed. "I will take that risk."

"I will not," Adela answered simply, knowing she was being unreasonable, but she could not suppress the twisting in her stomach. He was the chosen one. How could he make love to her and plan to marry another? Could... could she be jealous?

"Many lives are at stake. I must have peace."

"I will not give it to you!" she declared vehemently and pushed to her feet. "A woman's heart is not to be trifled with."

Phillip rose next to her. "I command you to give it to me!"

"Nae!"

"Guards! Take Mistress Adela to her chambers," he ordered. "I will not let you leave until I have the potion." He stood so close to her he could almost kiss her supple, stubborn lips. An uncontrollable force caused him to lean toward her.

"Then I will never leave," she whispered.

He felt her breath, sweet and warm. It had a powerful effect on his senses. For some reason his heart lightened to hear her say those words. Shaking his head, he turned away from Adela, eager to put distance from the lass who had him wondering if indeed he was losing his mind.

* * *

Phillip opened the oak door to his chamber to find a raven perched on the wide four-post bed. The bird jumped with fright and flew out the window leaving behind a long black feather fluttering to the ground.

Bending down, Phillip picked up the feather and studied it. This was indeed a day of unusual happenings. Shrugging his shoulders, he reached for the red wine on the side table and drank until his thirst was quenched.

He sighed with resignation. The meeting with Adela had not gone as planned. Why was she being so stubborn? Did she not see there was more at stake than his feelings for her? Phillip groaned and massaged his temples. His head pounded with painful jabs. Suddenly his eyelids became heavy and his vision blurred. His body heated with an unusual erotic sensation. He licked his dry lips and tugged at his tunic. Why did his clothes feel so tight?

Phillip stumbled to the bed and lay down. While ripping off his tunic, he used his feet to push off his boots, each one landing on the fur rug with a thud.

The room began to spin, and he felt light-headed and

ill. An overwhelming need to be naked hastened his fingers to undo his chausses. He was completely erect and his skin felt like it was on fire. He lay back into the bedding and closed his eyes, willing his mind and body to calm.

Blurred visions of a woman with raven hair and jade eyes swirled in his head. Her stunning features slowly became clear as she laughed and danced seductively in a red gown. Its material glowed like fire, caressing her body. She ripped open the gown, revealing her breasts and lifted each full globe to her pink tongue to lick. Then she raised her gown to her waist to show a marvelous thatch of black, curly hair.

Phillip's breathing quickened. He writhed on the bed, reaching out to her with a need beyond one he had ever felt before. He had to have her. He must have her!

She came closer and closer until she floated over him, yet did not touch him. "Do you want me?" she whispered.

"Aye."

"Then take me!"

He grabbed her hips and pulled her down to impale her onto his aching member. Her flaming gown settled around him, scorching his skin. Caring not that his flesh burned, he continued to plunge his cock inside her.

She fondled her large breasts and threw her head back while riding him like an animal. Her laughter sounded odd in his ears, like a cat's cry. Phillip was entranced with her beauty and the feel of his manhood while she manipulated its length, clenching her inner muscles.

She leaned down to look at him, but her dark, stunning face changed to Adela's youthful beauty. Sweet and passionate, she moaned with pleasure and smiled at him.

"I need you, my love," Adela said the words softly.

His body tensed and buried himself to the hilt. He wanted Adela more than any other woman. She cried her pleasure, bucking above him with abandonment while he groaned loudly, exploding within her.

Smiling with content, he reached up to kiss Adela; her earthy, nut-brown hair framed a face reflecting an expression of sexual exhaustion. Just before he kissed her, Adela's face changed back into the mysterious woman with sinister green eyes.

He lay back, confused.

She slapped him across the face and laughed before vanishing.

Complete darkness fell over his eyes and took him into oblivion.

When Phillip awoke from deep slumber, the early morning sunlight filtered through his window. He jolted upright in bed and found himself naked with warm juices on his satisfied manhood. Touching himself, he tasted the juices.

"Adela!"

Pushing to his feet, he quickly donned his clothes and opened the door. "No witch is going to enchant me!" he growled, and stormed through the hallways toward the guest chamber of the not-so-innocent captive.

CHAPTER SIX

"Hmm, Phillip is a good lover," Torella purred to her timid serving maid while she stretched before the full-length wall mirror. "But I am in need of a something more brutal." Tilting her chin up, she felt the presence of the raven before he swooped onto her window ledge and hopped into the chamber.

"Good eve, Master Dougal." Raising her arms, she faced the servant to help her lift the ruined ruby gown over her head.

The raven's cries echoed around the dark chamber as it transformed into a red-bearded man, masculine and naked.

"Good eve, milady," Dougal replied. He grabbed the servant's arm. Snatching Torella's sheer black nightgown from the girl's hands, he threw the garment on the floor.

"I rather think garments will just get in our way," he said, his voice husky with lust.

His hungry eyes roamed over the sorceress, her body firm and slender. She had satin-smooth skin and plump breasts with rose-tipped nipples, while the dark juncture of her thighs beckoned Dougal with the promise of paradise.

A wicked smile slid across Torella's exotic face. "Leave us." She dismissed the servant with a wave of her hand.

Her warm palm raked over his red hairy chest and she slowly rubbed her hips against his engorged flesh. "Did you take pleasure in watching me fuck your friend?"

Dougal closed his eyes, enjoying the effect her hands had on him. "Nae, it should have been me," he said, pouting, his red beard spiked over his upper lip.

"You must learn to share. My appetite is too great for just one man." Her hands slid lower to clasp his enlarged shaft. "And do you like your new power?"

"Aye, I do, milady," he whispered.

"E'ery time you take the raven's form, a bird dies to give you its life force."

"'Tis a small sacrifice," Dougal answered. His rough hands cupped her breasts while his thumbs rubbed her erect nipples.

"I agree."

Clutching his manhood, she led him to the bed and pushed him down. "Since you watched me having pleasure, 'tis only fair I watch you *having pleasure*."

Dougal smiled. "Aye, you have a lass in mind?"

"Lay face down on the bed and I will call in my servant," Torella said, her lips twisted into a smirk.

Turning over, Dougal laid face down, his thick hardness pressed into the black furs as he imagined having two women in bed.

The door opened and closed, but Dougal could not see the servant the sorceress chose.

Torella stood at the base of the bed. Her eyes glided over taut buttocks with a sprinkling of red hair and a hard chiseled back, delicious muscles formed from swinging an axe. She felt the familiar stirrings of dark magick filling her body, mingling with sexual desires. With the flick of her wrist, her lover's feet were bound to the bed by an invisible force.

"Why do you bind me, milady?"

"I would not want you to spoil my entertainment with your inhibitions," she replied, her tone dripping with disdain. "Take him," she ordered her servant.

Dougal twisted around to see the young male whose tryst with Torella he had interrupted. He held his huge erection and smiled with vengeful glee.

"Nae, I am not a woman!" Dougal roared, thrashing about, his buttocks remaining exposed.

"Come, come, now," Torella coaxed. "Do not tell me you have never wondered what it would be like to be plundered in the arse?"

Dougal remain quiet, knowing it was useless to deny it; she would only see through his protests.

Torella sat on the edge of the bed and ran her hands down his back. Her sexual, mystical touch burned his skin, its heat painful and pleasurable at the same time. Once touched by Torella, the cravings for more never ceased.

"My personal servant, Evan is an expert lover." She shifted her weight to lean over Dougal.

She sucked on his earlobe while her hands snaked across his backside. Meanwhile, the servant behind him lightly bit the supple flesh on Dougal's buttocks, slowly increasing his hardness once more. Using two fingers, the servant ran them down the cleft of Dougal's arse, playfully tapping the unyielding entrance.

Dougal moaned with yearning. Never had he felt this type of caress. His body throbbed for more. Hoping Torella would not humiliate him by making him beg, Dougal closed his eyes and enjoyed the erotic sensation.

Torella rose to her feet and watched, her luminous eyes shining with lust.

"Move aside," she ordered and came around to Dougal's back. Licking her thumb, she bent down and shoved it inside her lover. His guttural groans increased her arousal. Pinching her hardened nipple, she pushed in and out with the other hand.

Devil's maid! She was enjoying this!

Torella breathed in the sexual power Dougal emanated. Filling up her being, it stimulated her like nothing else.

"On your hands and knees, barbarian!"

Dougal's wrists and legs were released and he swiftly obeyed the command, eager for more pleasure.

Turning to Evan, she grabbed his large cock and guided it in Dougal's taut hole. Slowly it edged deeper while both men moaned in low, animalistic growls. The servant thrust his hips back and forth while clasping Dougal's shoulders.

Torella stood back and watched, licking her lips with delight. "Very good, lads."

Evan's balls banged against Dougal's backside. Torella's body glowed with a red aura, her muscles tight with sexual stimulation. 'Twas time she joined the men.

Lying down beside Dougal, she slid under him, allowing her legs to straddle his hips. Guiding his rigid flesh inside her, Dougal matched the rhythm of the servant, his face sweating profusely with rapture.

"Fuck me hard!" she screamed.

With his cock being milked inside Torella's searing core and his buttocks being plundered from what felt like a horse, Dougal barely held out until Torella found her peak. The moment her muscles tightened around him, he forcefully spilled his seed and bellowed so loudly the walls shook. Whether or not Evan initiated his own pleasure, Dougal did not care. He only had enough energy to drop to Torella's side and fall into a deep slumber.

The tangy smell of sex caused Torella's nose to wrinkle, and she swiftly rose from the bed.

"Bring me food." Torella dismissed the servant with a wave of her hand. Slipping into her black nightgown, the cool smooth fabric glided over her breasts and hips. She stood before the mirror and brushed her silky hair until it shone; satisfaction curled her lips.

She always hungered after stealing energy from the barbarian. So far Dougal was worth the trouble of keeping around even though he had irksome moments.

Snoring came from her bed and she glanced at Dougal's peaceful reflection in the mirror. "One day I will tire of you, and then I will have to kill you," Torella said, her tone matter-of-fact. The snoring became louder and she blanched at the offending sound.

"One day very soon."

With a threatening flick of her finger, Dougal was shoved onto his side as if a mule had kicked him. He grumbled in his sleep but did not wake and the room was filled with silence once more.

Returning her attention to her image in the mirror, she smiled with delicious thoughts of Phillip's superior, smooth body. Blue eyes changed to green, they gleamed with longing and her body shifted restlessly, eager for more sex.

"Perhaps the handsome chieftain will last longer than his elder friend." She licked her salty finger. "Until of course, I have used every drop of energy the laird possesses." No matter the size of her lovers, they had one thing in common ... they never lasted long.

* * *

Phillip dismissed the two guards outside Adela's chamber with a curt nod. No doubt they had fallen asleep during the eve when Adela sneaked past them to enter his room. He opened the door without knocking and stormed into the large chamber. The sunrise had not yet touched the west side of the castle, and while the meager fireplace did little to warm the dim chamber, heat stole into his body.

After a moment his eyes adjusted to the darkness. In two long strides, he stood before the elaborate high bed, the pale blue linen curtains tightly drawn. Clutching the material, Phillip shoved them open, unsure of what to expect.

Taken aback, Phillip took a quick sharp breath. Against his will a smile stretched across his face. Lying before him was an angel sleeping in peaceful beauty. Her glossy brown hair feathered over the pillow and long eyelashes rested sweetly against pink cheeks. Her chest rose and fell evenly beneath a white nightgown; even though it covered her primly, somehow it made her slim outline unbearably enticing.

The smell of berries wafted up to him, sending a carnal vision of her slender form riding him, her eyes pierced with lust. Sweat broke upon his upper lip when his member filled with blood and hardened. He pivoted and stormed to the window.

"Get a hold of yourself," he admonished and took a gulp of air.

"My laird?" a sleepy voice said from behind.

Phillip closed his eyes, willing his fervor to cool. He heard a rustling of covers, then small footsteps padding across the stone floor, yet he refused to face her. He did not need to see Adela's tempting vision to know she would be breathtaking.

"Is there anything wrong?" she asked.

Phillip sighed and turned, his traitorous eyes consuming the simple beauty of the exceptional lass. She licked her pink lips innocently and tilted her head with confusion, adding to her appeal of purity. Phillip had to resist her allure or take her in his arms and plunge his tongue past her lips. Abruptly, he turned his back on her. Why did this slip of a girl have such an effect on him? He must get a hold of himself!

Adela touched his shoulder. "Is there something amiss?" she asked again.

Phillip turned to her once more and she stepped back from the fierce scowl on his face. He was about to speak when the early morning light passed through Adela's nightgown, outlining her naked form beneath the simple material. Phillip cursed aloud. As if he needed any more encouragement. Even the sun was against him.

"Is there a reason why you are in my chamber so early?"

"Aye." He cleared his throat. "You bewitched and seduced me last eve," he accused, choosing to ignore how ridiculous he sounded.

"I do not understand," she replied. "I have not been out of this chamber since you had me locked in here."

"Somehow you escaped, came to my chambers and then made love to me." He refused to back down from his claims no matter how absurd they sounded. He knew what he saw and what he felt. "If you wanted to fuck, you did not have to put a spell on me!"

Adela winced from his crudeness, but he would not apologize.

His heart tightened.

Nae, he would not!

After a long pause she said, "I thought you did not believe in witches."

"Do you deny you were in my chamber?"

"Aye! 'Twas not me. Perhaps you dreamed." Adela's eyes squinted with annoyance and she stepped away from him.

"Nae, 'Twas you! I even tasted your essence on my—"

Adela gasped and backed against the bedpost. "How do you know what I taste like?"

"Well, I ... I..."

"You do not!"

"I know what I saw, felt, and tasted!"

"And I told you 'twas not I."

Phillip's gaze lowered and he stared at the hem of her nightgown. The shadows of the room covered Adela's naked outline and still his body responded with heated ardor. His eyes burned with lust. "I suppose there is only one way to know for sure."

Adela's hand fluttered to her neck while a becoming blush crept across her cheeks.

"You must be jesting," she whispered.

"Nae. If I am to sleep at night, knowing I do not have a witch under my care who wishes me ill, then I need to know 'twas not you who enchanted me."

"I tell you 'twas just a dream, naught else," Adela said hastily and slid around to the other side of the bedpost, the smooth mahogany beneath her hands offering her small protection.

Phillip remained still, his eyes narrowed with determination. "I will not do anything you wish me not to, but I will remain suspicious until I know for sure of your innocence."

He made to leave but Adela grabbed his arm. "Then I will allow you to taste me," she offered. "If that is all you will do."

"Aye, lass. If that is all you would like me to do," he drawled. His voice was low with promise of pleasure.

Odin's balls, nae!

She wanted more, much more. But knowing he wanted another to be his wife, another to share his bed ... she looked away from his probing gaze. It would not be right to make love to him. But since she awoke to find the man who filled her dreams standing in her chamber, she wanted to throw herself into his arms.

The man was too handsome by far. His golden hair framed a strong jaw and thick lips were made for a woman's kiss. He was all male, and her ripe body reacted primitively. She wanted to mate with him like no other man she had met. Let all her rules of honor be damned. She needed him. Needed him to touch her, kiss her, and to love her.

"Lie on the bed, lass. I pledge I will make this enjoyable," he vowed.

Adela swallowed hard and nodded, hoping her vulnerable heart was not exposed through her eyes. She lay on the bed and shivered with anticipation. Never had she been tasted by a man in such an intimate way and probably would never be again. If only she could stop shaking from the wanting.

"I will not hurt you," Phillip said, concern lacing his voice.

"I know."

Lowering himself to his knees, he slowly edged the nightgown up her thighs, exposing her most sensitive area nestled between her legs.

Adela's hands shook and she grabbed the blankets to stop them from fidgeting. Her chest became tight as her lungs burned for more air. She closed her eyes and released her shyness to Phillip's intense perusal. His warm hands traveled provocatively up her legs, heating the blood within.

She heard him sigh with appreciation, causing the tightness in her chest to shift lower to her abdomen, then on to her groin. Adela giggled to herself, thanking the stars for sending Phillip such a peculiar dream, one that caused him to kneel at her bed.

He kissed her inner thighs; his warm tongue swirled in circles, causing her to almost leap out of her skin.

"Hmm, you taste divine," he said, his tone totally masculine and erotic.

Adela's pulse quickened with every kiss he placed on her legs, edging closer and closer to her moist center.

"Do you like this?" he asked and licked the tip of her swollen bud protruding from between her inner lips.

"Aye." The tingling ache increased, making her body squirm with wanting.

She arched toward him, tipping her hips and he did not disappoint. Placing his hands on the outside of her thighs, he ran his tongue from the base of her pulsating core to her tender nub, licking her juices as if he had been starved for years.

Adela writhed in torment, her languid muscles stirring her to open her legs wider, giving Phillip better access to the place that yearned for fulfillment.

She entwined her fingers in his wavy blond hair, her other hand brushed across the tips of her receptive breasts. Adela's eyes focused on the stone ceiling above her, his muffled groan filling her ears.

"Dear Goddess," she whispered. "Do not stop." She moaned with a sound she was unfamiliar with.

His tongue plunged in and out of her and then centered on her sensitive spot. Adela's head swung from side to side, wondering how a body could hold so much pleasure and not die.

He eased his finger inside her and she ached again with incredible ecstasy. Her blood rushed through her veins, building an unbelievable passion within until she cried out in a dazzling explosion.

Phillip felt Adela pulsating inside, massaging his finger while his tongue enjoyed the smooth, moist essence. She came with shattering intensity, her whole body trembling. She was the most sensual woman he had the honor of pleasuring. Even now, the musky smell and taste of her on his lips drove him wild with desire to bury deep inside her. Nevertheless, he gave his word he would not go further.

Torment weighed heavily on his limbs. He rose to his

feet and sat on the bed beside her. Tenderly, he pulled her nightgown back down her legs, giving her a sense of modesty once more.

Still breathing heavily, she asked, "Know you it was not I who visited your chamber?"

"Aye, I knew in the first moment of tasting you."

"Yet you continued?"

"I could not resist enjoying the results my tongue gave," he said, his tone self-assured.

Adela smiled, arching an eyebrow. "In sooth, I enjoyed it too."

"As you can see," he motioned to the lump beneath his kilt, "I ache to slide myself inside you, but I am a man of my word."

Perhaps Phillip was the man to father her child. But the vision of her death outside these walls ... how soon would that happen? Adela glanced away, her eyes unfocused by thought. Mayhap it would not occur in the near future; in her vision, she was not large with child, so she might have already had the babe and passed on her legacy before being condemned to death.

Picking up her hand, he placed a chaste kiss on her skin. "Until next time," he murmured his voice rich with sensual meaning.

"Wait!" she cried out. "Do not leave."

CHAPTER SEVEN

She leapt from the bed and placed a hand on his arm, her fingers wrapped around the dark fabric of his sleeve. The warm, hard muscle flexed and Adela exulted in his male strength. Making a baby with this man would be a sinful pleasure. "Let us try again."

Phillip chuckled. "That is an odd way of putting it."

Clearing her throat, she said, "I mean, let us enjoy each other again. It would not be right for the laird to go without his pleasure." She reached up to place a kiss on his lips, but he pushed her away.

"I do not need your obligation." His mouth pulled into a firm line, his arms crossed.

She suppressed a giggle at his dark, serious features. Adela flicked her hair back, and lay sidelong on the bed to prop herself up on one elbow. She granted him, what she hoped was an alluring glance, and then lifted his kilt to expose his glorious manhood. Bold and thick, it stood to attention.

"You need not do this." He scowled.

As if his protestations would turn her away.

"Believe me…" She lowered her head, and slid her tongue down the taut, smooth skin and then back up to the wide tip. "… I want to do this," she purred, her eyes half closed. With one last look at his beautiful eyes, she opened her mouth wider and swallowed his cock all the way to the back of her throat.

"By Jupiter," he growled.

She wrapped her tongue around the head and repeated the action again and again. Phillip fell onto the bed beside her, surrendering himself.

"How did you learn…?" he panted, his eyes rolling back as his body sizzled with erotic sensation.

Adela licked the tip of his head and smiled. "I like to watch couples mating." She sucked on the sensitive head again. "I was on my way to the lake when I saw a maid take a man's penis like this, and since then I always wanted to do the same."

Adela swallowed his length again and pulled out. "Do you like this?" she asked, enjoying the salty taste from his cock in her mouth.

"Aye."

Cupping his balls, she worked her mouth up and down while watching his body stiffen with pleasure. His mouth dropped slightly ajar. The black woolen tunic stretched when he arched forward. Unable to resist, she reached her hand beneath the coarse fabric of his tunic. His warm torso was tight and sculptured.

To bring such a powerful man to a point of abandonment gave Adela a surge of possessive ecstasy. She wanted to savor every drop of his molten juices, but her need to have his baby had to take precedence. She needed his dominant seed inside her, giving her a strong life force to hold her legacy. Who knew when she would have another chance at making love?

Phillip groaned with agonizing pleasure. He was close…too close. She stopped and threw her legs over his hips, guiding his moist cock inside of her.

She leaned over his chest and he lightly bit the tender skin of her neck, sending shivers down her body. His cock bucked inside her, spearing her with frenzy.

His strong arms snaked around her back and sat them both upright. His breath fanned across her face and he shrugged out of his tunic and hugged her close. Intimately connected to him, her breasts pressed tightly against the hard wall of his chest.

She continued to grind her hips in a circular motion and felt his thick cock rubbing against the sides of her inner passage.

"A curse on you, Phillip, for feeling so good inside," Adela whispered, her tone filled with surrender. She tilted her head, her silky hair brushed against her back.

Phillip bent his head to fully lick her breast from bottom to top in one long motion. An intolerable pleasure shot throughout her body. The coarse material of his kilt gathered around his thighs, rubbing against her sensitive bud each time he thrust with his hips.

Breathing in short, painful gasps, her body plunged over the crest, shattering in exquisite sensation.

Suddenly, shrill laughter entered the chamber, echoing around the bed. Adela pushed against Phillip and rolled to the side. He rose and searched the chamber. The haunting sound grew louder and louder.

Adela pulled the covers up to her chin, her skin iced with fear. "Evil spies upon us again."

Phillip looked back at her. "Where is it coming from?" He went to the window and leaned outside, and then opened the door to find the hall empty.

The laughter turned to screams of torture, piercing Adela's ears. Squinting, she covered her ears and yelled, "Sun, earth, moon, I summon the Goddess Triana. Banish the evil from my chamber!"

Silence.

Phillip glanced around, then sat on the bed. "What just happened?"

"You better go."

"That was the same laugh I heard in my dream." Phillip leaned closer to her. "You know more than you are telling. Keep no secrets from me, witch."

Adela rose and promptly dressed, her face heated, both from their recent lovemaking and her rising fury. "I know as much as you do, and do not call me a *witch* in that tone."

Phillip shrugged into his tunic with jerky movements, his eyes blazing with anger and sexual frustration. His manhood, erect and aching stood beneath his kilt. "If you have brought wickedness into this abode to wreak havoc on my people, I will ..."

"Will what?" She faced him, her hands on her hips. "You were the one who brought me here, remember?"

Phillip studied her face, as if searching for answers. Pivoting, he roughly pulled the door open and slammed it behind him.

Adela sighed. Her chest ached with resentment and regret. Rubbing her arms, she collapsed on the bed. Without Phillip's overpowering, masculine presence, the warmth in the chamber had quickly vanished.

* * *

Phillip rushed downstairs and outside toward the village well. He grasped the rigging, his muscles strained as he pulled the heavy water bucket higher. Disregarding the cuts his hands received from his impatience, the bucket crashed onto the top bar and water sloshed over the edges. He grabbed the container with both hands, and in one motion tipped the cool water over his head, saturating his body with a shocking chill.

Sniggers came from behind, and Phillip turned to see a group of soldiers laughing at his uncomfortable state.

He shrugged his shoulders.

"At least it worked," he offered by way of explanation. They nodded in understanding and returned to their training. Phillip slicked his wet hair from his forehead, and returned without hurry to his chamber for fresh clothes.

After unwrapping his kilt, he dropped the long fabric and it pooled around his damp boots. Insistent images of Adela naked on the bed caused his blood to heat against his chilled, damp skin. He growled with frustration and ripped his tunic off, throwing the shredded fabric to the ground. She enchanted him with mystical dancing and dreams, and he fell for her charms like a lovesick youth. He must resist the witch's lure of seduction and remain focused on the pledge he made to his grandfather. An alliance could only be had if he used a love potion on Lady Torella.

Pensively, he leaned against the windowsill and looked below to his beloved, sleepy village. An ominous feeling gripped his chest ... Adela was a danger to his plans of peace.

CHAPTER EIGHT

After falling into an exhausted sleep, Adela woke up mid-afternoon to find the room bright with sunlight. She rose sleepily from the bed and dressed into her old gray kirtle. A wave of apprehension swept through her while she ran her fingers through her messy hair. Something was not right about Phillip's dream.

On bare feet, she padded to the door and opened it with abrupt force. Adela waited for the guards to prevent her from leaving, but when she peeked outside, the hallway remained empty. She shrugged her shoulders, stepped into the hallway, and closed the door behind her.

Pulling a small leather bag from her pocket, she dipped into an orange powder and blew the substance down the hallway. A sweet floral scent wafted up to her and she breathed deeply of the powder's soothing aroma.

"Show me where the laird sleeps," she commanded.

The powder floated along the stone floor like a snake and slithered toward the stairs. Adela walked up a steep spiral stairway and was led toward a room at the top of the tower. The cloud disappeared beneath an imperial oak door with an iron handle.

Placing her ear to the door, she listened for anyone inside. When all was quiet, she opened the huge door and entered the empty chamber. The powder swirled like a dust cloud over an immense bed.

"Thank you, please return."

The powder floated toward her outstretched hand, returning to the leather bag.

Tightening the binds, she replaced the bag in her pocket and glanced around Phillip's chamber.

"This is definitely his room," Adela said aloud. Two magnificent swords hung crisscrossed on the wall above the Roberts family crest, a fierce lone wolf framed with silver metal. She could almost hear the distant howl of the beast.

She inhaled the laird's personal scent of power and masculinity. His energy flowed around the chamber in colors of blue and green only Adela could see. Every object had the residual glow of his touch.

Adela stopped mid-step.

Every object glowed, except one.

She edged closer to a table by the window and ran her hand over two leather wristbands, a sharp dagger, and a metal chalice, most of its contents gone. The malevolent energy chilled her hand.

A black shadow hovered over the goblet. Adela picked it up and sniffed the remaining liquid.

"Belladonna! The devil's herb."

She dipped her finger in and tasted the tip. Blanching, she recognized the distinct hallucinogenic herbs of cowbane, mandrake, and monkshood.

The door crashed opened against the stone wall and she jumped.

"What are you doing in here?" Phillip asked, his eyes darkening with accusation.

"I ... I ..."

"Answer me!" In a few long strides, Phillip stood close to her, his hands firmly gripping her shoulders.

"I...You have been drugged," she blurted and tilted the chalice.

Phillip looked down and frowned.

"You drugged me?"

"Nae, not I," she responded with indignation and shoved the goblet in his hands. Stepping away from his close presence, she added, "Your wine was drugged with a potion known to few witches and made with rare ingredients. If given too much, you would be dead."

"Nonetheless, you seem to know of it," he replied, arching an eyebrow.

"If you wish for me to leave, I will."

Phillip closed the distance between them and placed a hand on her cheek. "Nae, I wish not for you to leave." His voice was low and soft. "I just do not understand why someone would go to the trouble of giving me erotic dreams."

Adela gazed into his eyes, hypnotized by the pure blue color and his utter beauty. His caress was soft and intimate, soothing the hurt she felt from his accusations. She leaned her cheek into the palm of his hand and closed her eyes.

"Adela?"

"Hmm?"

"I need that love potion."

Scowling, Adela pushed away from him and walked to the window. The tranquil view overlooked the entire village toward the green valley below. The loveliness did not appease her anger.

"I have a duty to protect my clan. I must have the potion, Adela." Phillip walked up behind her and placed his arms around her waist.

Leaning her body against his, Adela eyes became heavy. The heat of his chest burned through the thin fabric of her kirtle. He had only to touch her and her heart melted, stealing her anger and replacing it with an emotion she did not recognize. She only knew it felt so right to be in his arms as if they were born to be standing together.

She sighed, torn with what she should do.

"Is there no other way?" she asked, seeking the hopeless answer she wanted to hear.

"Nae. Lady Torella would sooner plunge a dagger in my back than to stop this feud with an alliance." Phillip kissed her neck. "I wish I was someone different. Someone who was free to …"

Adela turned in his embraced and placed a finger over his mouth. She did not want to hear what could not be. Her heart could not take it.

Slowly, he leaned down to claim her mouth. His tongue was searching, yielding and thorough, exploring the insides of her mouth.

Phillip pulled slightly away from her and his name was torn from her lips.

"Come, I wish to show you something," he murmured against her mouth and lightly kissed her again.

With his hand entwined in hers, he led her through the castle and then outside.

Walking down the pathway through the village, the laird stopped, greeting each passerby. Adela was amazed that he knew all their names, and they welcomed him as if he were close family instead of their ruler.

A precocious small boy ran around a woman carrying a baby. Phillip ducked down and lifted the mud-stained child into the air and then tucked him under his arm.

"How goes your day, Mistress Mary?" Phillip asked.

Jiggling the fussing baby in her arms, she smiled and answered, "I am well, thank you for asking."

"Does Seamus sleep well now that he is home?"

"Aye, 'tis good to have my husband back, although he grumbles about the daily chores."

Grinning, Phillip turned. "Adela, this is Mary, she is the wife of my loyal clansman, Seamus. And this grubby, fine lad is Patrick." Phillip set the giggling boy down, and he ran off.

"Ah, but Mary's pride and joy would have to be this darling lass, Isabel." His hand pulled back the blanket to reveal a smiling angel with a mop of curly, red hair and a mischievous smile to match her brother's."

Adela nodded and smiled. "I am pleased to meet you all."

"And I, you," Mary answered. "I crave your pardon, but this little one has a mighty appetite and searches for supper."

"Then you must away." Phillip bowed.

Patrick edged around his mother's skirt and returned Phillip's gesture, and then waved with earsplitting goodbyes.

"They seem charming." Adela lifted the hem of her skirt and stepped over a puddle.

Phillip pulled a violet flower from a nearby bush and handed it to her. "They are."

She accepted the fragrant blossom and smiled. It was the first gift she had ever received from a man. A simple gesture, but one she blushed from. Her attention was caught on the delicate petals; no other flower could match its beauty.

Unaware of Adela's heated face, Phillip continued, "Mary's husband is one of my finest warriors. He fought in our last skirmish with the Campbell's. The same clan Lady Torella sent to slaughter our neighbors and take their land." Phillip kept walking as if he discussed the weather.

Adela's hands dropped her side. "So Mary's husband could be killed the next time the Campbells go reiving?"

Phillip turned.

"Aye. We are usually called out to protect the borders every other week." His hand rested on the hilt of the sword strapped across his hip. "Many of the women you see here had husbands or sons killed while protecting these lands."

Adela surveyed the quaint cottages lined along the cobblestone road, and was sad for the men, women and children who had lost so much. She looked at Phillip. So much responsibility sat within his hands. No wonder his eyes were troubled when he looked at his people.

Adela bit her bottom lip, and reached out to touch his shoulder. "I will make—."

A scream rented the air.

Phillip and Adela rushed to the end cottage along with most of the village. Phillip pushed through the crowd and entered the small abode with Adela closely behind.

On the chair sat a young girl with black, straight hair and freckles. Tears fell down her cheeks. Her frantic mother observing the bloody teeth marks on the girl's ankle.

"What happened?" Phillip asked.

"The...the dog bit me," the little girl sobbed between gulps of air.

"Curse that damnable dog!" the mother snarled. "This is the second time he has bitten Edina."

"Mommy, do not hurt him. He was just playing," the little girl cried.

Adela crouched near the lass and inspected the wound. Behind her, she could hear Phillip explaining who she was to the mother.

"She's a witch!" the mother exclaimed, and the on lookers gasped.

"I am." Adela rose proudly, waiting for the mother to attack her. When no one moved, she continued, "This bite is deep and you will need my help if you do not want it to fester."

The mother captured Adela's hand, her winsome face lined with worry. "I welcome your help."

Adela curtly nodded, and pulled her bag from her pocket. She dipped her fingers into a green leafy poultice and crouched down. "This is summer savory. It will draw out the infection."

Applying the herb, she looked up at the brave child and smiled. "It will keep insects off you, too," she said lightly and touched Edina's button nose.

Edina giggled, releasing the strained energy within the room. Adela heard the people behind her sigh with relief.

Adela finished cleaning the wound, gently wrapped a cloth around the leg and tied it into a knot.

"Thank you so much," the mother said and threw her arms around Adela's stiff form.

Once released, Adela nodded. "You are ... most ... welcome," she said, unused to such warm attention.

The crowd cheered and Adela frowned in confusion. She glanced at Phillip and he stood to the side with a big grin on his face.

Finally recognizing her discomfort, he broke up the crowd and told them to go back to their duties, assuring them Edina would be just fine.

Adela turned to the lass. "Stay off the leg, and perhaps play with a friendlier dog."

"I will." Nodding, Edina's curls bobbed.

Leaving the cottage, Phillip and Adela made their way toward the castle when men and women came out of their homes to give Adela gifts, food and cups of ale.

Phillip laughed at her shocked expression with each kind word, and soon her arms were filled with many offerings.

"Here, let me take those," he said and unloaded Adela's arms.

"Why are they being so nice to me?" she whispered from the corner of her mouth.

"You helped one of their own."

"I have helped many people, yet they still hunt me mercilessly."

Phillip stopped walking and stared at her. His lips thinned and his eyes blazed with anger. "That will never happen here," he said. "I would sooner gouge out the eyes of the ignorant pig who taunts you."

Adela stepped back to Phillip's violent reaction. Who are these people? She had traveled near and far, and never had she found a tolerance for witches.

As if reading her mind, Phillip declared with an edge to his voice, "My grandfather use to teach his people that only a fool would fear the unknown."

"Your grandfather was wise."

His smiled. "Aye, he was."

They entered the darkened great hall and Phillip gave her gifts to one of his men to deliver to her chamber. Leading her over to the fireplace, they warmed their hands before sitting down to supper.

Adela turned to Phillip, unable to suppress her concern. She sighed. "I will need the herbs, mallow, caraway and lovage."

Phillip raised an eyebrow. "Why?"

"To make the love potion," she replied with quiet resignation.

His eyes softened with relief. "My most hearty thanks, Adela."

Nodding sadly, she added cryptically, "Know that there will be consequences to this potion."

"I understand." Phillip rose to his feet and left. He stopped mid-step and returned to Adela. Picking up her hand, he kissed her palm. "Thank you, again."

She watched his retreating back, his stride, brisk and animated as he went in search of the herbs.

Her heart whispered, *"if only you were as eager for my love."*

CHAPTER NINE

Torella cackled with glee at the vision of Adela's sad face in the scrying bowl.

"Will she make the love potion?" Naked, Dougal sidled up behind her to cup her breasts.

"Aye, she will make the potion." Torella pivoted and knocked his arms away from her. Preoccupied, she opened the doors to her armoire. "I must pack everything."

"Why do you need a love potion? The chieftain wants an alliance, and like all the others, he will fall in *lust* with you the moment he observes your beauty," Dougal said, his tone laced with jealousy.

Twirling around, she faced him with hands on her hips. Her voice hardened, "Lust is not love." She shot him a cold look and returned to her armoire.

"Let us not quarrel." Dougal shifted closer to her and placed his hands on her hips, rubbing his erection between her buttocks. "I am hard again, Torella. Let's fuck again before packing."

Torella turned and pushed him with unnatural strength clear across the chamber. His bulky frame slammed against the opposite wall.

"I am going to be the laird's betrothed!"

She pointed a long black fingernail to the window, her eyes glowing with swirling red flames. "Fly back to Gleich

Castle. Make sure nothing happens to the witch."

Dougal's eyes flashed with fury, but he remained silent. Within moments he transformed into a raven and flew out the window, his cries echoing in the distance.

Torella yelled for her servants and three scurried in, their heads bowed.

"Pack everything!" she demanded and went to a golden chest hidden beneath her bed.

Dragging it along the stone floor, she placed the heavy strongbox on her bed.

"Give me the iron key that holds my treasures!" she chanted to the box, her ruby lips curved into a half smile.

Within moments, a heavy copper key appeared in her open palm. Tapping the lid three times, a keyhole materialized. She inserted the key and opened the chest. Inside, the shadows held vials of liquid brews and dark spells written on old yellow parchments, along with jewels and gold coins befitting a powerful sorceress.

She picked up a small, empty vial attached to a silver necklace and unscrewed the lid. With a sharp fingernail, she sliced open the creamy skin on her arm. Hot blood dripped into the vial, filling it with her life force.

"Give me the bottle that holds Angelica herb."

Torella ran her hand over the box and a black vial rose. She uncorked it and swirled the dark liquid contents, then sniffed the sweet scent of musk. Tipping three drops of thick syrup into her blood vial, she sealed the lid and placed the chain around her neck, allowing the cool steel to rest between her breasts. She ran her hand over the vial, her lips widening to a sneer. "Now I am immune to the witch's love potion, while my enemy will foolishly fall in love with me."

A male servant rushed by her chamber and her cunning gaze jerked to the doorway. "Sex slave!" her silky voice echoed down the hallway.

The dark, knavish and alluring servant entered the chamber and bowed.

"How may I please you?" Cinnamon eyes flashed with hunger, his gaze roaming her naked form.

Torella raised her bloody arm, a single red line traced down her skin.

"Lick it," she ordered.

Without hesitation, he obeyed, sucking her wound as if he drank the sweetest of wines. She tilted her head back and laughed.

He lifted her into his arms and lay her down on the bed. Like most men, he was eager to taste more of his mistress. With the servants still packing in her chambers, Torella enjoyed a pleasurable eve of exploring her new black lover.

* * *

A light knock sounded on the door and Adela rose from the circle of herbs and candles scattered across her floor. Lifting a blue skirt up to her ankles, she carefully tiptoed between the ingredients of the love potion. She opened the door to find the well-groomed laird standing in the entrance, his eyes flicked approvingly over her while she matched his stare with one of her own. Opening his arms, he gathered her into them and kissed her soundly with a smooth face.

"I have missed your company this past day."

"I, too, have missed your charming dimples," Adela admitted and held him tighter. "And thank you for the new garments." She stepped back to swish the skirt of her gown. "They are most regal."

"It is you who makes them regal." He closed the door behind him.

"You do not need to say that," her tone, low and embarrassed. "I know I am not pleasing to look upon."

His fingers slid sensuously over her trembling chin.

"You are more beautiful to me than the full moon reflecting off the dark waters of our loch."

Adela went to pull away, but he held her fast.

"Please, never forget that."

She blushed and lowered her gaze. "I will never forget," she whispered and tilted her head up to stare into the flecks of his eyes. "I am glad you like the full moon, for this eve we need to visit her."

"Pardon?"

Reluctantly, Adela left his warm embrace and turned to the potion she had just finished. Lifting the glass bottle, she allowed Phillip to smell the tangy contents. "Slip this into Lady Torella's sweet wine and then drink immediately after her."

Phillip's nose wrinkled from the scent and Adela giggled.

"How will I get close enough to do that?" Phillip slumped on her bed.

Pocketing the potion, she bent down and picked up a green and purple candle. "I have added the same herbs to this wax along with the flower you gave me." Adela continued even though her throat constricted. She cleared it, trying to suppress her growing envy over a woman she had yet to meet.

"This flower holds your generous intent to seduce, while the herbs will call to Lady Torella's heart. But we must chant the spell and light the candle while standing in a body of water under the full moonlight." She looked up at his statuesque face, memorizing every chiseled feature. "This will bring her to you."

Phillip rose from the bed, his face heartrendingly dismal. "Adela, I want to say ..."

"Aye?"

"I want to say ..."

Adela moved closer to him, her body inches from his.

He sighed loudly and rolled his eyes upwards, his torment tangible to her. It did not take her being sensitive to his aura to know he did not like the situation they found themselves in.

"The loch is on the other side of the mountain," he finally concluded, both knowing it was not what he planned to say. "We can do the spell there." He placed a light kiss on her lips. "A part of me hopes that it will not work and witches are truly a story mothers tell their children to frighten them."

Adela nodded. Her heart breaking with each breath she took. For the first time in her life, she wished the same thing.

* * *

Hidden in the shadows and unnoticed by the two ill-fated lovers inside, a raven flew from its perch outside Adela's window. The bird's wide, black wings glided gracefully around the castle until he found an arched chamber window. Swooping inside, Dougal transformed into his full masculine height.

He shook his head, allowing his red hair to fall wildly around his shoulders. Dressing in a brown tunic and tartan kilt, he sat in a tall chair and tugged on his boots. With both elbows on his knees and resting his chin in his hands, he pondered on how he was going to survive without Torella's sensual touch. Already his body shivered with sweat, his muscles aching from the lack of her sexual contact. He had to get her back. He had to make love with her again.

Sitting upright, he massaged his prickly beard. A smile slowly crept across his face, a plan forming in his mind. If he slays the witch, her love spell would break, returning Torella's affections to him. It would break the alliance, and Phillip would be furious, but Dougal had no choice in the matter. Torella was in his blood.

He had to have her.

* * *

The hairs on the back of Adela's neck rose, walking through the thick grass toward the loch, but she shrugged off the feeling of doom. Surreptitiously glancing from beneath her eyelashes, she observed Phillip. The laird looked particularly tempting in a simple white tunic and kilt, his golden hair flowing gently in the breeze, a small sack casually slung over one shoulder. He turned to her and smiled, offering his hand to help her over a fallen log.

Adela placed her hand in his and her heart flipped with the heat of his touch. She wished he did not affect her the way he did. It would make casting the love spell a whole lot easier if she did not already care for the chosen one.

Moonlight illuminated the worn path to the glistening loch, but the surrounding forest remained cloaked in shadows. Ordinarily, Adela would stay indoors when it was only two nights before All Hallows Eve. It was well known that the beginning of the Celtic calendar created a thin line between the living and the dead. It was the only time her powers are greatly diminished. Her mother used to warn that all good witches seek shelter on All Hallows Eve, or else be met with an evil sorceress. She did not need to hear this more than once. Spawn of the Devil and his human mistress, sorceresses stole Celtic witches' powers by killing them. Adela never knew why they coveted good magick, but she stayed locked in her abode until well past Samhain.

"You are shivering." Phillip clasped her chilled hand close to his chest for warmth.

"I am fine," she offered, knowing it was only because he was close by.

"We are here." Phillip stood on the soft grass at the edge of the loch, the moon's mirror image reflected off the dark waters. He did not lie. It was beautiful.

Reaching into the coarse sack, he pulled out the candle and went to hand it to Adela when his eyes widened in shock. "What are you doing?"

Pulling the blue gown over her head, she stood before him naked, her nipples erect from the cool autumn breeze. "We need to have no constrictions on our body when casting this spell." She bent down and pulled off her slippers. "And I do not want to ruin my new clothes."

Grinning, Phillip offered no further argument. His eyes smoldered with wanting, and his body hardened with desire. She stood uninhibited in her glory as if she comfortably walked naked every day through the village. Her lack of coyness was refreshing and arousing. Phillip's gaze lowered to her beautifully formed breasts and he longed to flick his tongue across the stiff, rose-tipped nipples.

Adela retrieved the vial from her gown's pocket and gingerly walked into the chilly loch. Her perfectly formed buttocks gradually sank below the water until she stood waist deep.

"Light the candle and bring it with you," she called.

From out of a haze, Phillip hastened to undress and lit the candle with a flint from two jagged rocks. With a hand covering the warm flame, he entered the loch, mud squishing between his toes. His hardened member did not ease even with the cool water sloshing around his legs. In fact, it hardened with every step he took closer to the enchanting witch. Her long, brown hair barely touched the water, covering the round breasts he knew cupped perfectly in his hands. When first he saw Adela, he thought her to be a forest nymph, but now she resembled more of a mystical water siren, eager to lure him into the depths with her call.

Facing her, his muscles became languid. The candle's glow cast an orange tinge to the soft curve of her cheeks while the smell of softening wax filled his senses. Phillip wondered again if he was doing the right thing. He wanted his heart to call to Adela, not to a greedy, bloodthirsty aristocrat. He looked away from Adela's sweet, brown eyes. His chest constricted with an ache he did not like.

"Are you sure you want to continue?" she asked. "Once the chant has been spoken, yourself and Lady Torella will want each other with an unquenchable thirst."

"And what will happen to my feelings for you?"

"If it is lust you feel for me, it will disappear immediately. If it is love ..."

When Adela did not finish, he asked, "Aye?"

"If it is love, you will forever love two women until either one dies." Adela's glanced down at the candle, the smoldering flame reflecting in her moist eyes.

Phillip swallowed the lump in his throat and leaned toward Adela to kiss her. The taste of her sweet lips urged him to lovingly cradle her face. "Then I will love you until the day I die. But we must proceed." His eyes clouded with sorrow, his gaze lowering to the loch. "My people depend on this alliance."

A chill black silence surrounded them.

"So be it." Adela nodded with remorse and pulled his hand away from her face. She cupped his warm hands on the candle along with the potion. "Repeat after me." She gazed into his blue eyes, and continued, "I call upon the four elements of wind, fire, water and earth. Send my message to Aengus mac Og, the Celtic God of love and beauty."

Phillip repeated, his heart pounding wildly as a mist of water gathered around them in a protective cocoon.

Adela closed her eyes and tilted her head back to face the moon; a white ghostly light surrounded her body. She held the glass vial high in her hands.

"Hear us now powerful Goddess Airmed. We ask for your divine power to infuse this potion and bind this man, Laird Phillip Roberts to Lady Torella Campbell, with a love that cannot be broken."

A rose colored light snaked its way down from the stars and surrounded the potion, the ingredients glowing within. Adela released the candle and the light shot to Phillip and swirled around him, filling him with consuming warmth.

His ears rang with a loud beating of his heart. In the distance he heard Adela's soft voice, her tone filled with anguish. "Bring Lady Torella to her love and may they be happy in their life together. Blessed be."

As quickly as the light came, it departed and the water around them dropped to the loch, covering them in a light mist.

"It is done," the wistful tone in her voice sent prickly shivers down his back. "I wish you well." She blew out the candle, its smoky fragrance curled around her cheek.

She turned to leave, but Phillip placed a hand on her arm. "You cannot leave me," he said, his voice taut with sorrow.

"You must let me go! 'Tis cruel indeed to make me watch you marry another." Tears streamed down her cheeks, just to look at him caused her heart to ache. "Please, I beg you. Do not ask me to stay."

He paused to draw a breath to ease the pain within. "If you must go, then give me this time with you now, so that I may have memories of a love that was destined and not enchanted."

Tears ran down her cheeks and she pulled away from him.

"I ... I cannot."

CHAPTER TEN

Adela splashed out of the lake and Phillip followed. They dressed in silence, each in their own thoughts.

"Adela, we need to talk—"

"Nae!"

"You cannot leave."

"It would not work, Phillip!"

"Just give me one more night, give us one more night."

Adela's chest heaved with emotion. She could not look at him.

"Please."

A drop of water fell on her nose, coupled with a few more drops on her head.

"Come, let us away." He slung the sack over his shoulder and held out his long, calloused hand.

"I do not wish to return to your castle," she said, her voice barely a whisper.

"The rain comes. You must sleep somewhere tonight."

Releasing a sigh, she nodded and clasped his hand. Adela ran with him through the damp grass. Rain stung her eyes, blurring her vision. The heat of Phillip's tight grasp seeped into her hand, giving her the sense of protection while they battled against the elements. Even when they reached the castle, Phillip did not release his grip. Not until they stood at the entrance to his chamber, did he free her hand to open the door.

Soaking wet from head to toe, Adela shuffled into his chamber, the soiled edges of her gown sloshed around her muddy slippers. Phillip followed closely behind, and then shut the door. She turned to face him.

Golden hair dripped water down his angelic face while the tunic's damp material fit snuggly to his chest. He had never looked so utterly handsome than he did right now.

A cold voice in her mind urged her to turn away from him. Leave him to await his betrothal. Nonetheless, she could not do it. Her heart told her to stay, take whatever comfort she could before giving him up. It no longer mattered whether she had his seed growing inside her or the visions of her death. She needed him to tell her everything would be all right, even if it were a lie. Tomorrow she would face the harsh truth and be forced to leave him forever.

But tonight was theirs.

"Make love to me," she whispered.

He stood still as if waging a war of emotions within.

She swallowed past the lump in her throat, her hands fidgeting at her sides.

Is he now realizing the hopelessness of their love? Does his heart call to another?

"I am sorry. I should not have asked," she said.

"Nae, you should have not asked."

Adela went to leave, but he blocked her path. "You should never ask, because I will always hunger to pleasure you. All you need do is look at me, and I am your servant."

He pulled her roughly into his arms and kissed her hard on the lips, his tongue plunging into her mouth, branding her body to his.

By the Goddess, this man felt so good! *Take me*, she silently pleaded, her body thrumming with want. She pressed harder against his solid flesh, needing to be closer to him. Roughly she pushed away from him, and stepped back to rip off her wet gown.

She had to have him inside her.

Now!

He peeled off his wet tunic and unwrap the heavy kilt from around his waist. His hungry gaze never leaving hers. She took a moment to behold the hard contours of his superior male form.

A wicked gleam entered his eyes and he held out his hands. "Come to me," he ordered, his voice thick with wanting.

It was all the encouragement she needed to run and jump into his arms, her hands wrapped around his neck. With her legs straddling his hips, he effortlessly supported her weight by the back of her thighs. He reclaimed her mouth savagely, and her body melted with the scent of his passionate breath mingled with a musky scent of his arousal. Without breaking contact with her lips, he marched her over to the wall and pushed her up against it. In one swift thrust, he plunged his hard shaft into her willing body.

The vibration of his moan tickled her lips, sending shivers down her body.

He filled her core as he pushed in and out, a sense of urgency driving them both.

Enhancing the friction, she squeezed her thighs tighter, narrowing her inner canal.

He bit his lip and his eyes rolled backward.

Adela smiled with the satisfaction of knowing she could torment him as he tormented her. He increased his rhythm, thrusting his hips again and again. Unable to stop the wave of pleasure from overtaking her, Adela surrendered to the glorious moment. Her lungs burned for air, her body clenching with spasms.

Through gritted teeth, Phillip released a primal growl before spilling his hot seed into her. His whole body shook violently and he tightened his grip, holding onto her with fierce urgency.

When she no longer felt him pulsating inside of her, he released her, and she slid down his sleek body, damp with perspiration.

The muscles in her legs were weak from lovemaking. A sacrifice she was only too happy to make. She smiled up at him, he looked as exhausted as she felt and as completely sated. Adela picked up his hand and kissed the rough skin. "Come to bed before you collapse."

Breathing hard, he laughed and then whispered into her hair, "Believe me, my delicious witch, I have the strength to give you pleasure all night long."

He scooped her up into the circle of his arms and carried her to bed. Adela's gaze caught in his eyes and her heart leaped with renewed anticipation over the coming eve's activities.

* * *

A loud banging on the door forced Adela to push off Phillip's heavy arms from across her chest. She leaned over his sleeping form and smiled at the innocent boyish look upon his face. The door rattled again, this time more aggressively. Frowning, she shook Phillip.

"Wake up. There is someone at the door."

But he remained asleep. She tried shaking him again, but he did not budge.

"Phillip ..."

The door slammed open and three fearsome soldiers filed into the chamber. She screamed and shoved at Phillip's limp body once more.

"Die witch!" the soldiers snarled, then pounced on the bed and plunged each of their swords into her body.

Adela jolted awake in terror. Panting, she looked over at Phillip sleeping soundly beside her. She pushed away the matted hair on her face and swept her feet to the side of the bed.

"What purpose did that dream serve?" she asked in a choked voice, her gaze drifting to the sunrise outside the large window.

Adela released a long audible sigh and pushed to her sluggish feet. The cold stones against the soles of her feet chilled her naked body when she padded over to the washstand. Pouring water into a basin, she splashed the cool liquid onto her face.

A knock at the door echoed through the chamber. Adela jumped, a gasp escaping her lips. Her nervous gaze jerked to Phillip sleeping soundly in bed, and then back to the door.

"My laird," a male voice called through the oak. "An unusual guest waits below." He knocked again. "Are you awake?"

Adela went to the door.

"Do not answer it," Phillip whispered tersely.

Adela hesitated, blinking with confusion.

He struggled out of bed and pulled on a pair of breeches. Opening the door to a sliver, he leaned against the doorway. Adela heard his steward say Lady Torella sat impatiently in the Great Hall.

After Phillip closed the door, Adela asked, "Why did you not want your man to see me?"

"I wish not to tarnish your reputation." He lifted the lid of a timber chest at the end of the bed. "Looks like your spell worked in summoning Lady Torella."

"*You* wish not to tarnish *your* reputation," Adela hissed, ignoring his change of subject.

Phillip shrugged into a gray tunic and rubbed his cheek. "I did not want to share you just yet." He placed his hands on both sides of her face and kissed her lips.

She grimaced and leaned away. "Have you forgotten who I am? I can sense you are not telling the whole truth."

He ran his hand distractedly through his hair. "My people are going to have a hard time accepting their enemy as their mistress, even if it does mean peace. I did not want to confuse them with you being in my bed."

"You mean you did not want them to know their laird is bedding a filthy witch!"

"Adela!"

"Forget it."

She scooped up her soiled clothes and threw them on the bed. "I do not need your charity."

"You cannot walk outside naked," Phillip said and picked up the gown. "Get dressed and go to your chamber. I will be there shortly and we can talk about this."

Adela glanced away, her arms crossed. She was not going to wait like a dog waits for his master.

"Please, Adela. Do not leave without talking to me."

She sensed his inner torment. His eyes pleaded for her understanding.

"Very well." Adela snatched the gown from his hands. "Go tend to your new bride."

He gave a curt nod, and then reached into the pocket of her gown and pulled out the love potion. Pivoting on his heel, he left.

She flopped onto the bed with a deep sigh. What was she doing here? Was she prepared to be another woman in the laird's bed? To be forever hiding from his people? She sat upright, her stomach knotting with emotional pain. She had run and hid from people all her life. Afraid they would see who she was, afraid their fear of witches would kill her like her mother.

Clenching her teeth, she seethed with fury. She was not going to hide and she was not going to wait.

Shrugging into her gown and slippers, she slammed open the door and ran down the spiral stairway.

* * *

Phillip entered the Great Hall and met with a wall of tense silence. Several Campbells with hands rested on their sword hilts gathered around the high chair while his own sober clan remained poised and highly strung. He had only to say the word and the Campbells would be cut down before they lifted their swords from the scabbards.

Phillip stood before his own high chair. A barrier of bodies obstructed his view of Lady Torella. He raised his voice with command, "I am not accustomed to greeting guests through their army."

A harsh female voice responded, "Move aside, men."

The Campbells stepped back to allow their mistress to be seen.

Phillip peered hard at the dark beauty that sat imperially on his chair. Somehow, she seemed familiar to him.

Her long, angular face held high cheekbones and a slim nose, while thick, black eyebrows arched over jade eyes. Those same eyes stared at him with arrogant coolness.

Her expensive low-cut gown showed large breasts, and a trim waist. Lady Torella's body was made for the bedchamber, and Phillip guessed by the way her eyes devoured his physical form, she approved of him.

"I am here to accept your surrender," she said, her gaze probing further into his.

The word *surrender* echoed amongst his angry soldiers. They shifted with indignation. Phillip held his hand up to silence his men.

"The Roberts Clan does not surrender, but we do make alliances to strengthen our hold."

"The Campbells need no alliance. We are already strong."

"I do not wish to argue this point. Instead I ask you to consider what you would achieve by being the Roberts' allies rather than our enemies."

"What am I to gain?"

"You will gain joint power over the Highlands without losing anymore of your soldiers by our swords."

Lady Torella's eyes narrowed suspiciously. "What do you propose?"

"To become my lady wife, and end this feud once and for all."

She laughed and it sounded like a cat's call. That was how he knew her. The night he thought Adela invaded his intimate dreams. The mysterious woman was the very image of Lady Torella. Before he could ponder the implications, she interrupted his thoughts.

"I know not why I even bothered to come here. You have nothing I want." Lady Torella rose gracefully from the chair and stepped down from the dais.

"Before you go, let us leave on good terms." Phillip's men gasped behind him. "Bring me a chalice of sweet wine for Lady Torella."

She halted and then smiled like a cat that had licked a pail of milk.

A serving maid rushed over to Phillip and handed him a golden chalice. With the open bottle of love potion in his pocket, he turned his back on the Campbells and addressed his men. "With good faith, our clan will allow you safe passage through our lands until you reach the end of your journey." With slight of hand, he poured the potion into the goblet and then turned to Lady Torella.

"Drink in good health, milady."

She nodded and took a sip of the sweet wine. Her bejeweled fingers clutch the strange vial attached to a necklace around her neck. She handed the chalice back to him. "Now I wish to leave."

Phillip curtly nodded and stepped aside. He glanced at his clan standing along the edges of the hall, each one looking at him expectantly.

With a deep breath, he tipped his head back and drank the rest of the enchanted wine.

* * *

Adela returned to the guest chamber and gathered her bag of potions. She scanned the cozy room one last time before leaving. It was funny that this chamber was the only place she felt a sense of belonging. Even if it was brief, she appreciated the warmth it generated in her. Suddenly a sharp pain sliced through her stomach and she doubled over.

Something was wrong!

Rushing out of the chamber, she raced down the stairs to the Great Hall and paused at the last step.

Phillip's arms possessively wrapped around a woman's slender form, his lips kissed hers with the same passion he recently shared with Adela. The couple was unmindful to the shocked expressions of people around them. Her heart felt like it was being ripped apart. Adela could not look at the loving embrace any longer. She turned her gaze away to see the sullen trainer, Dougal, slink off into the kitchens. Unwilling to stay, she pushed her way through the soldiers toward the bailey door.

"Let me through please," she said to each person that blocked her path. "Pardon me, excuse me." Why would the not let her just leave? She wanted to scream at them to get out of the way. Tears blinded her vision, and she pushed past another man.

"Stop that witch!"

Adela gasped, and her head jerked up.

"Adela, do not leave!" Phillip called to her, but she did not want to turn to face him. The door was so close. Its light shined brightly through the passage.

"Adela." She did not need to turn to know Phillip was behind her.

He placed his hand on her shoulder and her body reacted against her will. She tightly squeezed her eyes shut and cursed herself again for falling in love with a man she could not have.

"Please stay."

Adela looked at the door once more and sighed. She turned and gazed into his eyes. Those damn beautiful eyes that spoke of his undying love for her.

Regretfully, she nodded.

"I will only stay for one day."

Phillip nodded and smiled with appreciation. "Come, I want you to meet her."

"Nae."

"Aye, tell me what you think of her. I value your opinion," he said, and led her further into the hall.

The huge room became silent, all eyes stared as the laird ushered Adela toward the crowd surrounding his highchair. Adela observed from beneath her eyelashes, knowing she would have a hard time hiding her jealousy to his betrothed. The Campbells opened a path for them to enter. Adela caught a fleeting glimpse of a dark shadow floating over the lady's head. By the time Adela lifted her chin the shadow had disappeared. Perhaps she just imagined it? Her emotions were raw after all. And the lady was more beautiful than Adela could imagine. The agonizing thought caused another sharp pain in her stomach.

"Let there be a great feast tonight!" Phillip shouted. "For this eve we celebrate the alliance of two great clans. May we forever have peace upon our lands."

People clapped without heart and then slowly left the hall, still confused by the sudden change in both Lady Torella and their laird.

Unconsciously, Phillip pulled Adela closer to his side when he introduced her to Lady Torella. They greeted each other with bitter rivalry in their eyes.

Regret assailed Phillip when he looked at Adela's forced smile. She did not deserve this betrayal of his heart, even if it was by their doing. He could not avoid the way he felt now. Lady Torella had swiftly become more and more important to him as the moments passed.

Yet he could not allow Adela leave. It was as if the very air would be taken from his lungs. He knew it was unkind to ask her to stay, but he could not help himself. Something told him to keep her here, by his side, safe and protected from the ignorant world outside his walls.

Lady Torella lifted her lily-white hand to Phillip, and he left Adela's side to help his betrothed rise from the chair.

"Let us be wed on the morrow, *my love*." Lady Torella looked down her nose at Adela and raised an eyebrow. "On All Hallows Eve."

Adela flinched and retreat a step. All Hallows Eve? She must find a safe haven to hide from evil that would seek her powers.

Phillip returned to Adela's side and entwined his hand with hers. His tender energy covered her like a warm blanket on a Scottish winter evening.

Nae!

She was not going to hide. Not on All Hallows Eve and not now. She leaned closer to Lady Torella so that only the exotic beauty could hear. "I just want you to know that I am going to fight you for this man."

The blacks in Lady Torella's eyes widened and then narrowed. With a cruel laugh, she replied, "You are welcome to try, Child."

Pulling Phillip's hand out of Adela's, Torella's voice purred with sensual provocation. "Show me to our marriage chamber. I desire to see if the bed will be suitable for our *lovemaking*."

CHAPTER ELEVEN

Every part of her body told Adela to run away. Run away from the heartache of witnessing Phillip with another woman. Run from the castle and hide on All Hallows Eve. Protect her powers.

Running was what she did best. It was what she was familiar with. But she remained in her chamber, staring out the window, her lips trembling and tears tumbled down her cheeks. What was she doing here? Why was she compelled to stay when this place held nothing but a tortuous vision of death and the misery of a love unrequited?

A light knock sounded at the door, and Phillip's soft timbered voice called out to her. Her heart leapt at the very thought of him on the other side of the door.

He was the reason she stayed.

Against her better judgment, she would walk through the fires of Hades to be by his side. She dried her cheeks with the back of her hand, and opened the door.

Black shadows etched under his eyes, and his usually smooth face held a day's stubble. He leaned one hand against the doorway, supporting his weight.

Adela wanted to throw herself into his arms but resisted the temptation, feeling unsure of her position in his heart. Did she have any right to his affections?

"Come in," she offered, her voice sympathetic to the

wretched look on his face.

"Nae, I better not." He straightened his back. "I hear you have not eaten anything."

"I am not hungry." Adela's chest became heavy with the dull ache of foreboding. "You did not come here to acquire after my health."

"Adela, I think you should leave."

She swallowed the despair in her throat. "You wish to see me gone?"

"Aye ... nae." Phillip ran his hand distractedly threw his hair. "I am being selfish in keeping you here."

"Please come in."

"Nae. I already feel like I am betraying my betrothed by being here."

"Phillip ..."

"This eve we have the Hand fasting and then on the morrow our nuptials will be read in the church. Please leave for the both our sakes, Adela. I fear I will not have the heart to go through with this ceremony if I know you stand close by."

Adela reached to touch his face, but he pulled away. The hurt and longing lay naked in his eyes.

"If you ever have need of anything ... anything at all," he said his voice raw. "Send a message, and I will be there for you." Turning, he left with a stiff back, his heels echoing on the stone floor.

A moan of despair escaped Adela's lips, and she softly closed the door. The pain of watching Phillip walk out of her life was too much to endure. How foolish she was. Thinking she could not only compete with the love spell, but with the exquisiteness of his betrothed. Lady Torella was breathtaking, and any man would surrender their sword just to get a glimpse of her.

Adela walked to the pitcher of water on her bedside table and looked at her image within the liquid. "I am ugly compared to her."

The vision in the water turned into Lady Torella's lovely features.

"Aye, you are ugly," Torella's callous voice taunted her. "Did you honestly think he would choose you over me?"

Adela gasped. Her shock replaced with anger. "He did not choose you! He chose peace for his people!" Adela yelled at the pitcher.

Eerie laughter filled the chamber, and Lady Torella's features disappeared.

Adela grasped the pitcher, the cool metal burning her fingers and threw it out the window.

"What just happened?" she asked aloud and flopped down on the bed, her brows tightening with thought.

Lady Torella had powers? But how had she missed the signs?

Adela cursed herself for not realizing sooner. The fleeting shadow that hovered over Lady Torella's head this morn, and the strange things happening to Phillip, it was too much to be mere coincidence.

"What are you up to, Lady Torella?"

If Adela went to Phillip with her suspicious questions, he would think she was jealous. She must find proof of Lady Torella's powers. Adela rose to her feet and snatched her leather sack from the side table before rushing out of the chamber.

In the hallway, she looked both ways to see if she was alone. Although everyone knew her to be a witch, she was used to keeping her powers secretive, a protective practice that would not fade overnight.

Shoving her hand in the bag, she pulled out a fist full of orange powder and blew the enchanted substance off her hand. Tying the bag to the red velvet rope around her waist, she ordered, "Take me to Lady Torella's chamber."

In the shape of a snake, the powder slivered along the stone floor.

Footsteps echoed from around the corridor and Adela stopped. She whispered tersely to the powder, "Drop!"

The last grain of powder dropped to the ground just before an old, short serving maid hobbled around the corner. Her keen blue eyes brightened when she recognized Adela leaning casually against the wall.

"Good day, Mistress Adela."

"Good day."

The serving maid's forehead creased with concentration. She shifted the weight of the bed sheets under one arm, her small slippers standing on the powder. "Do you smell that?"

"What?" Adela innocently asked, arching an eyebrow.

"That scent. It is," the maid sniffed the air. "It is ..."

"Heather."

"Aye, heather."

Adela laughed nervously and glanced down at her powder. "This time of year, the mountain air is filled with the sweet scent."

The serving maid nodded and took another step, squishing the powder into the stone floor. She went to leave and paused mid-step. "The villagers and I wanted to thank you for being here."

Adela tilted her head in bafflement.

The old woman continued, "'Tis been a long time since we have seen the laird without a frown across his brow. We all feel you do him well, unlike that...*woman* he is to marry."

Adela suppressed the tears that threaten to overspill. Choked with emotion, she could only nod at the woman.

The maid nodded in return and an awkward silence fell between them. The maid went to leave, but turned and threw her free arm around Adela's neck.

Adela stiffened and then relaxed in the woman's warm, tight embrace.

"I am sorry for the way things have worked out," the maid croaked. With a brisk rub of Adela's shoulder, she left as promptly as she had arrived.

Adela placed her hand over her mouth and watched the maid scurry away, the powder stuck beneath her slippers. Mystified over the villagers' acceptance of her, she shook her head in wonder. Did they truly like her? Other than Phillip, she could not remember the last time someone had touched her with acknowledgement.

A warm glow slid over Adela, a smile stretched across her face. No wonder Phillip would sacrifice everything for these good-natured people. Adela raised her chin a fraction higher. She was going to make certain his sacrifice was not in vain.

"Powder, reform."

The orange dust rose from the stone floor.

"Continue," she commanded and followed in its wake.

Adela walked through a series of hallways and stairs. She never realized how big the castle really was until now. Suddenly, the hair on the back of her neck rose.

She halted.

Someone was watching her.

She turned around and found the dim hallway empty, yet the ghostly chill that ran down her spine told her otherwise. She turned to follow the powder. The feeling of malice clung to her senses, its clammy smell fouling the air. Rushing her steps around a corner, she pressed her body against the wall. A wave of apprehension swept through her. What form of menace hunted her? She must gather the courage to look back. To see what she was up against.

Although the taste of bile rose in her throat, she swallowed a gulp of air and forced herself to peek around the corner.

No one was there.

A flapping noise sounded close to her head and she looked up. She screamed when a caw resonated in her ears. A large raven swooped down from the rafters and fluttered around her head, its sharp beak pecking her scalp, drawing blood.

Adela waved her hands above her head and ran down the hallway. Her powder having disappeared from sight, she ran mindlessly, flailing her arms to ward off the ear-piercing call of the raven and its vicious blows.

She barged through an open door at the end of the hallway and quickly shut it behind her. Leaning against the heavy oak plank, she breathed in shallow, quick gasps. Her pulse beat erratically as she tried to keep her fragile control.

After an interminable silence, Adela pressed her ear against the oak to listen for signs of the demonic bird. When all was quiet she turned to face the darken interior of the chamber.

"Why does that raven keep following me?"

A shadow appeared at the corner of her eye, and she jump in fright.

It was her orange powder.

The tight knot within her began to relax. She sighed on a shaky breath. Opening the bag tied to the rope around her waist, she whispered, "Return."

Adela stepped further into the chamber and was overwhelmed with a sense of evil, drugging her spirit with a heavy darkness. If the powder was in here, this chamber had to be Lady Torella's. Why did she not sense anything at their first meeting? Perhaps losing Phillip had distracted her powers.

The chamber held a large bed, similar to hers, but with dark blue blankets and sheer curtains draped from the posts. Adela surveyed the neat covers. Not a crease could be found.

A heat fused her cheeks when she pictured Phillip and Lady Torella tangled in the bed sheets, each clawing at the other with insatiable hunger.

"Stop it!" she admonished herself and turned her back on the bed. Her gaze was drawn immediately to a dark mist hovering over a golden chest in the corner. She kneeled down before the chest and found no keyhole. Placing her hands on the metal lid, a malevolent energy climbed up her arm, chilling her blood. An agonizing groaned escaped her lips. She resisted the sharp pain that seeped into her soul. With all her weight, she pushed harder against the chest, but the lid would not budge.

"Curse this chest!" Sitting back on her legs, Adela panted with frustration and absently rubbed her arms.

She studied the outside of the strongbox. The plain sides held nary a carving or drawing.

"It is unusual for a chest to have no creative symbols identifying the maker," Adela said, tapping her finger against her chin. "Perhaps it has already been cursed."

Opening the bag at her waist, she pulled out a black leaf and crushed it over the chest.

"I command you to take away the guardian and open this lid."

A dark green light exploded in front of her. Adela yelped and fell back. Putrid smoke filled the air, and she coughed while waving her hand back and forth to disperse the haze.

When the smoke cleared, she edged closer to find the lid open. She pulled out vials of potions and herbs, a jar of dead men's toes, a horse's hoof, and a bag of small animal bones. At the bottom of the chest lay a thick ancient book with *Dark Magick* written in gold across the cover.

The shock of discovery siphoned the blood from her face.

"She is a sorceress."

Against her instincts, Adela picked up the vile book and riffled through aged, yellow pages until she found the spell Torella used on Phillip to give him sexual hallucinations. Phillip had experienced no dream, but a reality. Torella had seduced Phillip that night. And it was done before Adela had even considered the love potion. Torella has spied on them all this time.

But why?

Why go to all this trouble when she could have made an alliance with Phillip without the potion?

Phillip. She must warn him.

Pushing to her feet, she rushed to the door and swung it open.

Blocking her path stood a large fierce soldier with red hair.

Dougal!

He grasped her shoulders in a painful grip.

"I want you to be a good witch and die quietly."

CHAPTER TWELVE

Torella exhaled as she walked into her chamber. "I suppose I will have to change my gown for the Hand fasting this eve." Untying her black cloak, she threw the coat on her bed.

"No matter what you wear, milady, you will always look fetching," Jacob said. Her new lover stood behind her and brushed her hair aside to kiss the back of her neck.

Torella swiveled around and smiled. Her new dusky slave had proven to be an adequate lover with plenty of sexual energy to feed from. She ripped his coarse gray shirt apart and ran her hand down his dark, smooth chest.

"I believe we have time before the feast to have one of our own." Torella placed a foot on the bed and lifted her black velvet gown to her waist, exposing a thatch of dark coiled hair at the apex of her thighs. "Now eat!"

Jacob dropped to his knees, grabbed her buttocks for support and pushed his thick, wide tongue past her outer lips. She choked on a moan. The familiar warm sensation seeped into her body, filling her spirit with power.

"This pleases me well," she drawled.

Holding his head firmly against her groin, she pinched an erect nipple beneath her gown. While his tongue swirled against her slick, satin flesh, Torella's arousal increased at the sight of Jacob's sable skin against her creamy thighs.

Once she was wed, she would see to obtaining a harem of these magnificent men.

She threw her head back, her body clenched with building pleasure.

"Aye, that's it! Keep licking!"

So close.

Torella smiled with anticipation. She glanced down at her slave and her smile faded.

"What is that?"

Jacob raised his head. "Do I displease you?"

Torella pushed him away and stormed around his sprawling body. "What is this chest doing open?"

Jacob shrugged and rose to his feet.

Lifting the lid, she ran her hand over the golden metal. "Show me who was in here."

A reflection of the witch appeared across the lid. In the vision, Adela opened the chest and searched through Torella's private possessions. The girl rose from the floor and went to leave. But Dougal stood at the door, his murderous eyes glaring at the intruder.

"Argh!"

A wave of black shadow descended the chamber and her slave cowered in the corner. Her eyes glowed red with mounting fury. The air crackled with tense energy when she stormed out of the chamber.

* * *

Ominous clouds gathered to the east while Phillip crouched low to study the condition of battlement's stone wall. The chestnut stallion shifted behind him, tugging on the reins in Phillip's hand.

"Repairs will need to be done this side," he informed two of his soldiers. A wild gust of wind tore at his hair.

His horse sidestepped against the whirling gale, his head bucked up and down. "Easy." Phillip rose and tightened the grip on the reins.

The eldest soldier with a thick blond beard asked, "Think you we need to repair the wall, since we now have an alliance with the Campbells?"

"Can never be too safe," Phillip replied distractedly, studying the darkened skies.

A young, lean soldier of nineteen winters questioned, "Are you having second thoughts, my laird?"

Phillip jerked his gaze to the youth. "Nae. Why would you say that?"

"It is just ..." he looked over at the other soldier who vigorously shook his head. Uncertainty clouded his brown eyes, and he remained silent.

"Go on, lad," Phillip urged, his arms crossed.

"'Tis just we were hoping you had changed your mind. A lot of the clan does not want a Campbell living among us."

"Lady Torella is ..." Phillip paused, his gaze unfocused. "Did you hear that?"

"Hear what, my laird?"

Lifting his weight into the saddle, he turned his horse around. "Something is amiss." His chest wrenched with an unfamiliar pain. Adela's fair image came to mind and his heart raced.

The horse dangerously galloped down the mountainside, his hooves sliding in muddy patches. Phillip used all his experience to keep his balance. He had not the time to lose his saddle.

Mud flicked up behind the horse's backside as they raced through the open gates, his people scrambling to get out of his way. Swinging from his mount, he ran inside the cool interior of the Great Hall and called out to his servants. "Has anyone seen Mistress Adela?"

A few serving maids stopped what they were doing and stared with blank expressions.

Growling with frustration, he rushed passed them to

take the stairs two at a time. His breath came in labored gasps by the time he reached Adela's chamber. He searched the empty room to find the few possessions she had brought with her, gone.

She left him after all.

He had hoped...

He shook his head. It broke his heart to see the hurt look in her eyes when he told her to leave. However, 'twas for the best. So why did he have the sense that Adela was in trouble?

"Macquire," Phillip called to a heavily built soldier passing in the hallway.

"Aye, my laird?"

"Who is on duty as Gatekeeper?"

"That be O'Malley."

"Summon him."

* * *

"Is this about the chicken I ate?" Adela tried to shrug her arm free from her captor's grasp, but he only tightened his hold.

A boisterous laugh echoed off the enclosed walls of the secret passage he had shoved her into. "I can see why Phillip is infatuated with you." Dougal leaned closer to her ear and she smelled garlic on his breath. "Even confronted with death you have a sense of humor."

She scrunched up her face and waved her hand across her nose. "I have seen my death. It will not come by your sword."

"Brave words you speak."

He pushed her into another passage and another spider's web.

"Why do you wish me ill?" She brushed the silky net from her face.

"Once you are dead, the love spell will be broken."

"It is Dougal, right? The War Trainer?"

"Aye."

"Then let's assume you have some sense about you." Adela abruptly snatched her arm back and turned to him. "Whether I am alive or dead the love spell would still be effective."

"You would say anything to save your life."

"Aye, usually I would, but this time it is true." Adela squinted through the darkness to see the color of his aura shift. "You are not in love with Lady Torella. She has enchanted you with lust."

"What makes you think I do this for her?"

"The energy surrounding you tells me it is so."

A vision flashed before her eyes of Dougal's head being sliced off, his blood soaking the fields.

"Listen to me, please. We must return. There is death for you ahead," Adela implored.

"Shut up!" He yanked her arm and heaved open a thick door at the end of the tunnel. "My plans will not be thwarted."

A gust of wind kicked up around Adela's gown, blowing her against the solid wall of Dougal's chest. He pushed her outside into a meadow full of fragrant heather and pine trees. The secret passage led them to the other side of the mountain.

Adela tried to convince him again. "You must listen to me."

"I do not care what you say. You will die, and Torella will be my lover once more."

"Nae, I will not!" A shrill voice called from behind, sending a shiver of fear through Adela.

Dougal's face went pale and he turned, pushing Adela before him as a shield.

"I told you to look after her, not kill her!" Lady Torella's black gown swayed in the blustery weather.

The sword from his scabbard lifted on its own accord

and raised high in the air. He released Adela's arm to defend the blow, but was too late. The sword sliced through his neck, severing his head.

Warm blood splattered on Adela's face and clothes. She stood still, her body numb with shock.

The fierce winds whipped ebony hair around Torella's face as she walked closer to Adela. The sorceress wiped blood from Adela's cheek with her fingertip and placed it on her tongue. "Hmm, taste like metal."

"What do you want with me?" Adela's voice wavered with apprehension.

Torella smiled with wicked green eyes and circled Adela like a predator playing with its prey. "I want your baby and then your powers."

Adela gasped and her hand flew to her stomach. "I am not …"

"Aye, you are! Phillip's seed grows deep within, mixing with your enchanted blood."

Adela yelped when Torella grabbed her arms. Within a blink of her eyes, they were transported to the castle's dungeons.

Adela forced back the nausea that threatened her balance. She backed away from the sorceress until she felt the damp wall behind. "Phillip would not allow you to kill me."

Torella threw her head back and laughed while caressing the vial resting on her chest. "Thanks to your love spell, Phillip would do whatever I ask."

"Why were you not affected by the same spell?" Adela's attention was drawn to the necklace. "That vial protects you."

"You are quick, lass." She walked over to the barred window and smiled down at the bailey below. "I simply love the smell of burning witch."

"Why are you doing this?"

"When you burn on All Hallows Eve, your powers will be transformed unto me just like the other Celtic witches before you."

Adela gasped. "You killed my family?"

Torella laughed without mirth. "Who do you think raised the suspicions of the town's people on All Hallows Eve?"

"I will not let you get away with this. I will find the power to fight you."

"No witch has been able to on All Hallows Eve. Although, 'tis delicious to watch."

Adela's eyes darkened with rage. "That will not happen to me."

"Aye, it will. Once the flames start to singe the skin on your feet, you will crumple with pain." Torella floated over to Adela and stood inches away from her. "I can smell your fear already."

Adela tilted her chin a fraction higher.

Ignoring Adela's bravado, Torella pivoted, her gown swirling above the soiled rushes. An expression of smug delight showed in her eyes. "There is one option that I suggest you take. You can either allow your baby to burn along with you in your womb, or drink this potion." A chalice materialized within her hand. "With your death, your babe's soul will enter my womb, to be brought up as my child, but with your powers."

"Dear Goddesses."

"They cannot help you now. This dungeon is cursed to bind your powers until All Hallows Eve." She placed the chalice on the floor and opened the dungeon door. Turning back, she added, "At least you got your wish, Adela. The MacAye bloodline will exist after you are gone. Each generation will give me their powers. My eternal youth and beauty will be assured."

"Nae, you cannot do this!"

"Drink the potion, Adela. Save your baby from burning to death, and Celtic magick will live on."

The dungeon door slammed closed. Adela jumped from the heavy echo. She rubbed the chill from her arms and looked out the window to the bailey. Sounds of hammering floated up to her prison. Torella's soldiers were building a base for the stake.

Her vision was coming true.

Her fate inescapable.

She will burn.

Leaning against the mossy walls, she collapsed to the floor and sobbed with desolation. Through the tears, her eyes flicked over to the chalice.

By itself, the chalice scraped eerily across the stone floor when it came to stop within arms length. Adela picked it up. Its lime liquid glimmered with hope. Tenderly, she placed a hand across her stomach. An overwhelming love radiated from her core being.

She was with child.

Phillip's child.

She knew what she had to do.

After wiping her tear stained face, Adela held the chalice with both hands.

"Phillip, wherever you are. Forgive me. I must save our baby."

CHAPTER THIRTEEN

Phillip's cool exterior depicted an ease he did not necessarily feel. He shifted with impatience on his high chair while overlooking the festivities. His lovely betrothed sat to his right, her cleavage full and enticing in a blood-red gown. Phillip resisted the urge to stare at her. Every time he did, his will melted in her sensual emerald eyes, urging him to give her anything she desired.

Instead, he chose to survey the room, his astute gaze leaping over the heads of countless people, seeking the familiar face of only one that remained elusive.

A warm hand glided up his thigh and a jolt of heat went through his muscles.

"What are you doing, milady?" he choked out the words, keeping his eyes averted.

Lady Torella whispered in his ear, "I want us to have an heir straight away." With one finger, she tilted his chin toward him, forcing his gaze to be captured within her almond shaped eyes. "Perhaps we could start this eve?"

"My laird," Macquire's deep voice called from a distance, slowly pulling Phillip out of the trance.

"My laird." The soldier's voice was closer. "Pray pardon for my interruption, but I have found the gatekeeper."

Phillip shook his head to clear it. But he did not miss

hatred emanating from the lady's eyes, while glaring at Macquire. The poor soldier lowered his head and stood to the side of Phillip's chair.

"Who did you find?" Phillip stirred from his seat and twisted around to focus on what his man was saying.

"O'Malley. The Gatekeeper."

Phillip stared blankly at the large soldier and then beyond to the elderly gatekeeper standing close to the wall.

"You ask me to find him immediately."

"I ... I do not know why."

Their puzzled expressions reflected his own as he searched his hazy memory of the afternoon. After a long pause, he cleared his throat and responded, "Go back to your duties. Wait—has anyone seen Dougal? He has not reported to me in some time."

Macquire shook his head, and O'Malley stepped forward. "He did not leave the keep, my laird."

"Very well, be on your way."

"Is something amiss?" Lady Torella asked. Her hand pressed against his groin, and his body thrummed with a voracious need for more than just her touch.

"Nae." He tightly closed his eyes and shifted back into the chair, pulling away from her hand and the overwhelming sexual power she weaved into his mind and body.

"Then let us away to our chamber."

Adela's sparkling eyes flashed before him and his chest assailed with a terrible sense of loss. "I must find her!"

"Who, exactly, do you need to find?" Lady Torella's eyes narrowed with jealousy.

"It matters not." He rose from the chair without looking at his betrothed. "I will see you in church on the morrow."

"I look forward to our alliance."

With a curt nod, he pivoted and left to find O'Malley. His thoughts cleared when he increased the distance between himself and his betrothed. He snaked his way through the crowd with a single hope.

Gatekeeper O'Malley would know where Adela had gone.

* * *

The dungeon door slammed against the wall and Adela woke with a jolt. She was amazed to have fallen asleep on the dank floor covered in rotten rushes. The overwhelming stench of rat droppings made her eyes water. Rising gingerly, she winced at the soreness her sleeping conditions had brought to her muscles. She rubbed her eyes to better see in the dark then groaned, wishing she had remained asleep and oblivious to her visitor.

The lady's crimson gown rustled while she paced back and forth in silent fury like a caged animal. The irony was not lost on Adela, since she was the one who sat caged in a dungeon.

Abruptly, Torella stopped and stared at her. "Never has anyone refused me."

Gradually, it dawned on Adela what her captor was talking about. She tried to suppress a satisfied smile, but failed. Her heart leapt at the thought of Phillip rejecting Torella's advances. "Perhaps you are not as enticing as you think."

Fury burned within green eyes of the sorceress, and Adela's smile faded.

Torella flicked her hand, and an incredible sharp pain tore through Adela's abdomen. Her face twisted with agony and she crumpled to the ground, her arms clutching her stomach.

Standing above her, Torella peered down with contempt. "Think you are woman enough to keep a man like that interested?" She flicked her hand again, and

Adela's head pounded, as if someone smashed a large stone into her skull, over and over again.

Adela refused to plead for her to stop. She would take this all day if she had to, but she would not beg.

After a long pause, Torella scoffed, "You bore me."

The pain vanished and Adela pushed herself upright, sweat beading on her forehead, her breathing labored.

She lifted her hate-filled gaze to find Torella's back turned and her focus on the empty chalice by the doorway. Adela swallowed, if she only had the strength to attack the sorceress. Even without the curse on the dungeon, she would still not have the ability to defeat her.

Torella had the power of all the murdered Celtic witches, along with the skills mastered by serving dark magick. If that was not enough, the enchanted vial on her necklace protected Torella. Adela's spells would be useless against her as long as she wore that necklace.

"At least you did something right," Torella purred, her fury dissipated.

Adela rose slowly to her feet and leaned against the wall for support. "I will do anything you want with nary a fight, just do not hurt my baby or Phillip."

"Laird Phillip? Now why would I want to share Gleich Castle and the Highlands with him? This is the strongest fortress in all of the land, and it will soon be mine." She crossed her arms over her chest. "Besides, the noble chieftain would not remain passive when I teach the dark arts to our baby," Torella smirked. "Well, your baby."

Desperate fury peaked to shatter the last of Adela's control. She pushed herself away from the wall and scratched Torella's surprised face, leaving four red welts across her flawless cheeks.

Torella's shocked eyes widened, placing a hand to her wounds. Adela reached for the vial, but an invisible force shoved her against the wall and the breath was knocked from her lungs. Her arms were pushed above her head and held tight, bound by invisible chains.

"No one has ever struck me!"

"No one has struck you. You have never been refused in bed. By Jupiter, you are not having a good day," Adela taunted.

"You just insist on being punished, don't you?" Torella stepped closer, and ran her hand over her wounded cheek, the welts disappearing. Her pink lips puckered while her gaze roamed over Adela's body. Her eyes changed in color from green to red, glistening with sexual superiority.

"If torture does not break you, perchance your desires will."

Adela did not like the sound of that. Why could she not learn the quality of silence?

Torella licked her lips and began to unlace Adela's gown.

"What are you doing?"

"I am intrigued to see what Phillip finds so appealing in you."

"Stop that!" Adela struggled against the unseen binds.

"Perchance you taste sweeter than cream?"

"'Tis not my body that keeps him from yours."

The sorceress continued unlacing the gown until it fell from Adela's shoulders. She cupped Adela's breast in her hands, feeling the weight of them.

"Then pray tell what is it?"

Adela gulped, her body reacting on its own accord, her nipples hardening with the caress.

"He loves me. That is why."

"He loves me too. Thanks to your potion." Torella dipped her head and her pink tongue darted out to flick Adela's erect bud.

"Stop that!" Adela growled, incensed that her traitorous blood flowed with arousal. Torella's soft hands were so warm, shooting an exquisite, wicked pleasure throughout her body.

Torella rubbed both Adela's nipples between her thumb and forefingers then ran her tongue up the side of her neck, sniffing Adela's hair.

"Mmm, you smell of berries."

Adela could no longer fight the enchanted feelings of ecstasy. Torella's warm breath tickled her ears, sending an unbearable ached between her thighs.

She bit hard into the sensitive skin on her neck, and Adela groaned with pleasure.

Torella gripped Adela's chin in her hands and pressed her body closer. "Your sexual energy is pure," she declared, and then captured her mouth, pushing her tongue past Adela's lips.

Adela used the last of her will power and shifted her face to the side. "I will never submit to you."

Torella cackled and lifted Adela's skirt, plunging two fingers into Adela's aching entrance. Adela's body jerked with a sexual craving, but she remained silent. She would not submit. She would not submit. Oh Goddess, it felt so good!

Lifting her fingers to her mouth, Torella sucked on them with relish. She stood so close to her, Adela could smell her own musky scent.

"You do taste sweeter than cream."

Adela closed her eyes, willing her body to resist the sexual spell the sorceress welded.

"Look at me."

Adela tightened her eyes shut.

"Look at me!"

The soft body against hers stepped away, leaving her blood heated and unsated.

A rich, masculine voice softly spoke, "Look at me, Adela."

Her eyes flew open to find Phillip standing before her, completely naked. He reached for her, but Adela jerked against her binds. "You are not Phillip."

"Aye, I am." He nibbled at her lips and ran his hands over her breasts. The unique scent of him invaded her senses and Adela wished with all her being that it was he. In dire need to be caressed, she would have given anything for him to be standing in front of her.

"Kiss me, Adela. I have missed you so." Phillip reclaimed her lips, urging her to open them up. "Kiss me."

The heat from his body clouded her resistance, demanding she surrender.

"I have missed you too." She opened her lips to him and received a long, drugging kiss.

His hands were all over her, roughly groping her body as if his life depended on their lovemaking. Adela no longer cared. She needed him with a passion that scared her.

Phillip lowered to his knees before her and regarded her with tempered eyes of longing. "Spread your legs for me."

Without inhibition, Adela obeyed. Her body was in pain. She needed release from the pent up passion.

Tilting his head, he plunged his tongue into her tender, moist heat. He swirled it with skillful ease, taking his time. Adela's breathing increased, burning her lungs. Everything around her disappeared, all her senses focused on the pleasure Phillip's tongue brought to her body. She wanted to live in this moment, this time and place of suspended ecstasy.

With that thought, her veins filled with liquid fire, and Adela called out Phillip's name, her body clenched with intense bliss. Her scream echoed around the dungeon.

How could she take much more pleasure?

She couldn't breathe.

Oh, but the pleasure ... when would it end?

She must calm down to breathe. Her body tensed, shattering again.

She growled through clenched teeth, the man between her legs unrelenting, dancing his tongue around her sensitive bud. Dear Goddesses, she felt so alive.

Keep going, she begged silently.

Aye, that's it.

Again her body shuddered, yielding to the burning hysteria.

She stood panting, her chest heaving. Adela went to wipe her hair, slick with sweat, off her face, but could not move her arms.

Reality of her vulnerable position washed over her like a cold bucket of water. Adela cracked open her eyes she held tightly shut from the sensations.

"Phillip ..."

He rose gracefully from the floor. His smile turned into a deep rumble of laughter. The peculiar sound changed to a feminine cackle. His image transform into Torella's sensual dark beauty.

Torella wiped the juices from her mouth. "You were delicious."

"Nae." Adela struggled with feeble strength. "How could you torture me so?"

"'Tis what I do best, lass."

"Phillip—"

"—is not here," Lady Torella gloated.

"Phillip," Adela continued, "will destroy you."

The sorceress laughed. "How sweet. You really think he is coming to rescue you?" Torella sniffed, and walked to the darkened window. Her eyes glazed with malicious anticipation. "Beyond those hills my army awaits my word. If your lover tries to save you or denies me a wedding, I will have his people slaughtered and his village burned to the ground."

Hopeless tears streamed down Adela's face. A chill crept over her body.

Torella returned to Adela's side and kissed her lips. "Still think he would choose your life over the lives of his entire clan?"

Adela snapped her head away. Her arms were promptly released, and she slumped to the floor.

Torella opened the door with a flick of her wrist and strolled through it, calling over her shoulder, "Do die with dignity. I wish not to have my wedding disturbed by your screams."

* * *

A knock sounded on the door and Phillip stopped his pacing.

"Enter!"

The door opened to O'Malley, and Phillip waited impatiently for the old man to shuffle into the chamber.

"What news?"

O'Malley coughed and then replied, "It has been two moons now, and we have not found either of them, my laird."

"This is not like Dougal to disappear. And how did Adela leave without a single person seeing her?"

"May I suggest, my laird, you try to forget about them and hasten to the church. Your betrothed looks to be a lady who is not used to waiting."

"Aye, you have the right of it." Phillip ducked his head and slid on a chest banner with the Roberts' colors of black and green. Brushing down the thick material with his hand, his thoughts centered on his grandfather. Today he would solidify his pledge to the old chieftain and create a peace between the two warring clans.

So why was he so miserable? This was what he had wanted after all.

Distracted, he passed O'Malley standing in the doorway, then halted mid-step.

"Send two soldiers to Adela's home again and another two to search for Dougal outside the keep."

"Aye, my laird."

* * *

The eve of All Hallows brought with it a crisp breeze. The wind whirled in a spine-chilling song outside the church. Within the holy walls, a restless clan sat on the pews, each vying for an advantageous view of the doorway and the missing groom.

Phillip opened the double doors, and silence fell. His heels echoed upon the stone floor as he walked down the isle to stand next to his beautiful bride. Her exquisite gown of emerald velvet matched her green eyes. Torella's face was hard with annoyance at having to wait.

Phillip's throat ached with sorrow, his stomach clenched with the sense of dread. Everything was wrong. He could feel it in his blood. How can he marry Lady Torella when his heart was with Adela?

The priest began the ceremony with an open prayer, and his betrothed touched his hand. A sensual energy surged through his body, blurring his vision and distorting the words of the priest.

He stared into her eyes.

Time suspended while his mind slipped into a deep trance.

CHAPTER FOURTEEN

The sun had long since set, leaving a cool breeze to brush Adela's hair while she rested her face against the dungeon window. Did nobody notice the Campbells building a stake in the back of the bailey? Surely some questions would arise even if everyone were busy preparing for the wedding.

Adela sighed, but it did not release the aching knot in her chest.

She sat on the floor and pulled a chunk of rushes out from beneath her. Scrunching her face, she resisted the temptation to glance down at the stiff lump of fur she had moved. How could Phillip keep his dungeons in such a state? He obviously never came down here. However, after two days in the dungeon, the smell of old urine no longer bothered her. She wished she could say the same about her stomach. The only substance given to her was a tankard of dirty water shoved into her hands by a silent Campbell soldier.

All Hallows Eve was upon her along with the familiar weakened state her body and soul suffered. Her powers were diminished. She could not even manage a spark for a candle to light the darken cell. Thoughts of Phillip came to her mind, including the insistent regret of all the things she wished she had said to him. Now it was too late.

Too late for her, but it was not too late for Phillip or his people. She must find a way to tell Phillip that Torella is evil. Perhaps on her way to the stake, they would pass someone and she could yell to them to stop the wedding.

Heavy keys scrapped in the lock and the door rattled. Adela pushed herself up against the wall. She would not meet her fate with sobs or regrets. She may be afraid of burning to death, but she did not need to show her captors. The cell door opened and a bright orange candle illuminated three Campbell soldiers with grim, bearded faces.

One of the larger soldiers seized her arm and led her out of the dungeon. His deep voice sent a chill down her back. "If you come meekly, witch, I will kindly chop off your head after you are dead, so that you may go before God to be judged accordingly."

She scoffed at his ignorance. Why fight stupidity? Let them do to her what they wished. It only mattered that she warn Phillip of Torella's plan before she died.

The Great Hall was deserted and so was the bailey. Everyone within the village attended the wedding ceremony. Adela spent her whole life running from people, and now when she needed them around, they were nowhere to be seen.

Adela walked around the castle wall to the bailey. Several Campbells circled the stake, no doubt eager to watch the witch burn. Her gaze traveled the length of the tall wooden structure to the dry timber surrounding its base.

Her heart fell into her stomach. Fear gripped every muscle in her body, paralyzing her completely, rendering her unable to take another step.

The soldier shoved her onward and she fell, grazing her knees on the jagged stones. Rough fingers bruised her arm as Adela was pulled to her feet and dragged to the stake. The solider leaned his fat belly against her to tie her arms behind her back. The smell of onion on his breath made Adela gag and her eyes water. She forced her gaze upward to the starry sky while icy fear wrapped around her heart. No wonder the MacAye women had not been able to concentrate and use their powers. She was terrified!

Despite how much she resisted them, tears streamed down her cheeks and her body trembled. Courage left her side the moment she saw the stake up close. Everyone had told her to accept fate, die quietly and with dignity. But she did not want to die.

She wanted to live!

She wanted to feel her soft baby in her arms, and to be safe within Phillip's loving embrace.

She would not accept this fate. Her destiny was to love Phillip and have his child. Why else had she been led to him? The chosen one.

"Do you have any words of redemption, witch?" the soldier asked, a flaming sconce in his hand held precariously close to the wood.

"Aye," she shouted. "I call to the ancestors of MacAye. Help me now to live! I beg of you!"

The soldiers laughed and each one set light to the wood. The crackling of burning timber filled her ears, the flames licked hungrily towards her feet.

Adela tightly closed her eyes and said aloud, "Stay calm, Adela. Stay calm." She peeked down at her feet. "The fire is so close," her voice rose with hysteria, "what tree burns that fast?"

Heavy, black smoke filled her lungs, and she coughed. Her burning eyes watered from the smoke that curled around her like a heavy blanket.

"Control your fear. Control your fear," she chanted. She would not die today, no matter what she was taught by her mother. The thought of her mother brought images of her burning golden hair, her screams of pain vibrating in Adela's ears.

Bile rose to her throat. She mustn't think of her mother. Not now. She would change her fate. She had one thing her mother did not.

A Celtic baby within her body made from the love of the chosen one.

Perhaps if she could channel the baby's new power, it would give her enough magick to contact Phillip.

Sweat poured down Adela's face, the heat from the flames warming her exposed skin. Her pulse raced erratically and her chest heaved with overwhelming panic. She had only moments left.

"Remain in control." Adela squeezed her eyes shut. "Phillip needs me. His people need me."

Focusing on the baby, holding the infant in her arms, Adela absorbed the love it generated within her. Slowly, a small amount of power returned to her, filling her body with energy. "Phillip, hear me now. Seize the vial around Lady Torella's neck. Take it!"

* * *

"Halt!" Phillip commanded.

The church filled with noise from his people commenting with speculation.

"What is amiss?" Torella asked, her tone laced with frustration.

Phillip's head filled with Adela's frantic words. His gaze went to the vial lying against Torella's alabaster skin. "I cannot marry you," he said.

"Hear me well, Phillip!" Torella spat. "Either you marry me or my army will slay your people."

"I will not, Lady Torella." He snatched her necklace and broke the chain around her neck.

Shouts of "huzzah" loudly filled the church, his people cheering and patting him on the back.

Phillip rushed to the door, Adela's faint cry for help tugged at his heart. He burst outside into the night, the wind whipping his clothes.

The aroma of burning wood floated on the breeze.

Without knowing where he was going, he ran toward the smoldering scent. Adela's screams echoed in his head, urging his legs to carry him faster. His heart stopped for a beat when he ran around the castle to find Adela tied to a wooden pole, flames only moments away from her tender flesh. He saw her panic-stricken eyes and rushed forward only to be held back by two Campbell soldiers.

He struggled against them, fighting each with all his might. With the thought of Adela dying, his muscles gave him extra strength. He will not fail her.

"Phillip, hurry!" she screamed.

He pulled the sword from the scabbard at his side and sliced through both soldiers only to find more coming his way.

He had no time for this!

Dropping his sword he leaped over the flames and stood face to face with Adela. The fire began to creep up his boots, singeing leather to his skin. Suppressing the searing pain, he untied Adela's wrists from the pole.

"Phillip!" She pointed at the flames igniting her gown.

Using his bare hands, he slapped the fire out on the scorched material. He lifted her into his arms, and leaped over the burning wood. Not releasing her until her feet were on the ground once more, he held her tightly within his embrace. "I thought you had left me."

"Phillip, I—"

Adela was interrupted when several Campbells stood before them with angry faces and swords drawn. The largest of the men came forward. "Our mistress will not be pleased. We have orders to kill you both."

Phillip's gaze went to his sword lying in the flames

beyond his reach. Cursing his luck, he pushed Adela behind him and waited to be cut down. He had only to stall the soldiers until his clan found them, hopefully before they get to Adela.

The Campbells stepped forward and Phillip knew he had no defense. His whole body tensed, waiting for the sword's sharp point to penetrate his chest.

From somewhere behind, a stone was thrown with deadly accuracy on the face of the advancing soldier. Another issued and then another one. Phillip looked over his shoulder to find Adela picking up stones and throwing them with all her strength.

The Campbells retreated, defending themselves as best they could with their hands. Smiling to himself, he bent down and helped fight the vicious soldiers with simple stones.

The Roberts guards appeared behind them and swamped the enemy within moments.

Phillip dropped his stone and turned to Adela. Without hesitation, he lifted her into his arms and swung her around. After returning her to the ground, he captured her mouth with his own.

He pulled away to make certain she was not harmed. His eyes lovingly roamed every inch of Adela from her face to her feet. "I am impressed with your choice of weapons."

She grinned, brightening her face. "Thank you."

O'Malley pushed through the crowd and stood before Phillip.

"You have news of Master Dougal?"

"Aye, he has been found without his head."

The villagers gasped.

"Who did it?" Phillip's eyes darkened with fury.

"I did!" Torella screeched from behind the crowd.

Everyone stepped to the side to allow a wide path, fear

etched on their faces. The lady's scarlet eyes glowed unnaturally. She stormed closer to Phillip and Adela. "You foolish knave. Your friend betrayed you all for a simple power."

"Dougal thought himself to be in love, and you killed him," Adela retorted.

"Love can be fatal," Torella crooned.

"Seize her," Phillip ordered.

With a swipe of Torella's hands, Phillip watched everyone in the bailey clutch their throats, gasping for air.

Phillip was the only one not affected. He turned to Adela and held her shoulders. She doubled over, wheezing.

"Release them at once."

Torella laughed. "Why would I do that?"

Phillip's heart wrenched. His people were suffering.

"Please, I will marry you. Just lift the curse."

Torella swayed her hips, sidling closer to Phillip.

"I will allow your people to live if you throw the witch back into the flames."

"Nae!"

"Kill her or they will all die."

He looked at Adela and her face started to turn blue. He narrowed his eyes at her lips. She whispered something, but he could not hear.

Lowering his head, he asked, "Adela, what is it?"

"Neck…necklace. Destroy the necklace."

Phillip searched his pockets to find Lady Torella's necklace.

Holding it up, he watched the range of emotions on the Torella's face go from smug arrogance to fear.

He threw the necklace to the ground and crashed it beneath his boot, spilling the bloody contents between the stone cracks.

"You stupid dolt," Torella roared.

Adela chanted beneath her breath, so low only Phillip

could hear a slight murmur.

His people began falling to the ground, the very breath taken from their lungs.

Torella laughed with mirth at Adela. "You have no powers witch, it is All Hallows Eve."

Adela rose upward, gulping a big mouthful of air. The rest of Phillip's clan did the same.

The cool breeze soothed her lungs. With her hands on her hips, she faced Torella. "The eve has reached its zenith and a new day begins."

"Nae!" Torella stepped back. "My army awaits my word, they will burn everything! Everything!"

"I think not." Adela reached forward and grabbed both Torella's wrists. She stared deeply into her eyes. "I call upon the love of my unborn child. Take back my ancestor's powers from this sorceress."

"Nae, that is not possible. Your babe belongs to me. You drank the potion!" Torella shrieked, her face slowly changing with age.

"I tipped the foul liquid out the window. My baby belongs to me."

Torella tried to struggle from Adela's grasp, but she held tightly to the old woman's wrists.

Older and older she became as her body hunched over and her looks faded into wrinkles.

"Nae, my beauty, my youth!"

"You will never execute another Celtic witch."

Torella's body slowly disintegrated, her once flawless skin falling off, leaving only bones behind.

Adela held the wrist bone until it changed into dust. She opened her fist and blew the ashes into the wind. "May your soul be free of evil, Lady Torella."

The villagers shouted with joy and mobbed Adela with gratitude. Adela shoulder's stiffened and she tried to relax and accept the well wishes. Large crowds still made her nervous, but she knew Phillip's friendly clan meant her no harm.

"Step aside," a commanding voice bellowed over the numerous heads.

Phillip pushed his way to her side and held her hands.

"Adela, is it true? Do you carry my babe?"

She nodded and smiled at the unadulterated pleasure shining from his angelic blue eyes.

Phillip folded her into his arms and kissed her. Pulling away, he raised his voice for everyone to hear.

"I love Adela MacAye, and I plan to marry her." Phillip looked over his shoulder. "If anyone has a problem about having a witch for a mistress, speak now."

The dying crackle of the nearby fire was all that could be heard.

Adela's eyes moistened from the villager's warm acceptance of her.

"Adela," Phillip turned to her in his arms. "Will you do me the honor of sharing your life with me? With …" Phillip gestured to his people, "all of us."

"Aye, my laird. I will." She looked over at his people, and then returned to face the chosen one, her true love. "The honor is mine."

EPILOGUE

Adela woke in Phillip's embrace, his naked hard body pressed against hers. Memories of the erotic night before invaded her mind. She sighed wistfully and reached up to kiss Phillip's beautifully, sculpted lips.

He stirred awake and smiled. Adela's heart skipped a beat. Phillip had to be the most handsome man she had ever met. And he was *all hers*.

"Good day to you, milady wife."

"Good morn, my husband."

Phillip stretched, his chest muscles twisting while he yawned. Adela bit her lip, the familiar stirrings of longing fluttered within her stomach.

"You have that glint in you eyes."

"What, pray tell, is *that glint*?"

"A wicked one." Phillip kissed her neck.

"Speaking of wicked, is Lady Torella's army still camped nearby?"

"Nae, they left shortly after we returned her soldiers on your request. I still think we should have punished them for trying to kill you."

"Peace needs to start somewhere."

Phillip growled affectionately, "You are wise for a wicked woman." He ran his tongue up the side of her neck to her ear, and Adela moaned with pleasure.

Phillip propped up on his elbows. "I want to do something for you."

"Oh, believe me, husband, you are doing it. Cease not."

He grinned, his dimples melting her heart.

"Nae, I mean something special for saving my people."

"Well…there is something you could do."

She leaned over him and whispered into his ear.

He bellowed with laughter, merriment dancing in his eyes. In one swift movement, he rolled Adela over, his body on top of hers.

"For you, my love, I will clean the dungeons myself."

THE END

Read on for a sneak preview of book two in the Celtic Witch series, *The Celtic Witch and the Sorcerer*. Available February 2008, from Resplendence Publishing.

CHAPTER ONE

"Your daughter is dead!" the midwife announced while looking down at Gavenia's lifeless body on the bed.

Floating in the corner, Gavenia's spirit denied what she was seeing. She shook her head at the vision.

Nae, this cannot be happening. I do not want to be dead!

She observed her mother standing at the foot of the bed. Lady Adela MacAye looked so sad, like the very heart was stolen from her chest. Tears streamed down her mother's round cheeks, her brown eyes frozen to the depths. "She can't be dead."

The midwife lovingly touched Gavenia's ashen face, yet Gavenia did not feel a thing. No caress, no warmth. Only her spirit remained alive in the chamber room.

The midwife intoned, "I am afraid the birth of her child was too much to bear."

Her mother pushed the midwife to the side and threw her arms around Gavenia's shoulders. She rocked back and forth, chanting, "I am so sorry, I am so sorry."

Gavenia moved with silence behind her mother. No

one could see or hear her, but she still wanted to touch her mother's slim shoulders. Comfort her in some way.

The oak door crashed open and Gavenia jumped.

A stranger charged into her chamber. His tall, muscled stature crowded the small room and the occupants. Sweat beaded across his aristocratic face as if he had run through the halls of Gleich Castle to reach her side. Scraping of metal echoed through the quiet room when he drew his sword from the scabbard. His tormented eyes brightened with an unnatural glow while the stranger studied Gavenia's peaceful face.

Did she know him?

Adela growled at the intruder, "How dare you bring that weapon in here. My daughter is … is …"

"She is dead." He accused, "and you killed her!"

Gavenia opened her eyes and rubbed the perspiration from her forehead. Her heart pounded with anxiety. She inhaled a gulp of air and then released it.

Another death vision.

The muscles in her back ached. She raised her arms above her head and moaned while stretching to relieve the tensed knot. Being a Celtic witch and foreseeing her own death was not a power she wished to have.

Rising from her fur-lined chair, she replaced the stone runes she held in her hands into a sable, drawstring bag. She sighed, and collapsed back into her chair, her cream gown billowing around her ankles as she lifted her legs and hugged them to her chest. Ever since she turned three winters old, she had been burdened with the same vision. Equally distressing, she learned that she was duty bound to procreate like a cow in the pasture. One of the last Celtic witches, her family demanded she produce a child to inherit her powers of good magick. Yet, when her time came to give birth, her death vision foretold she would die. It did not inspire Gavenia to seek the *chosen one*, the one man that could sire a babe to carry her ancestral powers.

She would rather be alone for the rest of her life. At least she would have a life.

Gavenia lifted her thick hair above her neck, allowing the cool breeze from the large arch window to caress her warm skin.

A light knock sounded at her door.

"Come in," she answered and rose to her feet.

Her older brother, Callum, entered and absently sat upon her discarded blue robe on the bed. "I bested Father in chest last eve. You should have seen his face." He chortled, "The mighty chieftain beaten by his son."

Gavenia stared at her brother of twenty-two winters. Like her, he was the water reflection of their father. His angelic features, long blond hair and square jaw line stole many maidens' hearts. But what endeared Callum to all was his carefree nature and kind blue eyes. The future chieftain of the Roberts clan was the first born of a Celtic witch and Highland laird. Callum's charm was irresistible, making it hard for Gavenia to stay angry when he teased her.

Gavenia tugged at the garment beneath her brother. "Get off my robe."

Her brother shuffled to the side and she snatched her robe from beneath him, replacing it in a long jeweled chest at the foot of her bed.

"You are in a foul disposition this morn. Did you have another death vision?"

"Why do you ask?" she snapped.

"You are always moody afterwards."

"You would be too if you saw your death over and over again."

"Why not tell me of this vision. I will do all within my power to see you are kept safe. As future laird, I will protect you with a thousand soldiers."

Gavenia smiled. "I wish not to burden those I love with this knowledge. And besides, some things even you cannot protect me from."

"Mother's death vision did not come true. Perhaps the same will be for you."

"Mother did not see herself dead, only the beginning of her torture. I have seen my corpse."

Callum rose and pulled her into his arms. "I am sorry that your powers are a curse as well as a blessing."

Gavenia pushed him away. "I wish not to think of it."

"You are right. Let us rejoice in the moment. It is all we have." He jogged to the door. "Prepare yourself. Mother seeks an audience with you. She has news of my betrothal and wishes to throw a feast in celebration of the alliance," his voice rose in a melodious tone, "and now she hopes to snare you a husband."

Gavenia groaned and turned her back on her brother. The door he closed behind him muffled his chuckles. Just what she needed: more pressure from her mother to find the *chosen one*. She would have to put her off. So far she had reached twenty winters without her mother forcing the subject. She knew her time was running out. Soon she would have no choice but to accept a man's betrothal.

It was not fair.

Her life was spent behind the protective walls of Gleich Castle. Her family denied her every opportunity to explore the world, saying it was unsafe for a witch in these times of superstition. Only the Roberts clan accepted the Celtic witches as good instead of evil. Outside, people were not so knowledgeable and their ignorant fear had caused her grandmother's death.

It was only a matter of time before she was wed and on her way to producing the next Celtic witch.

She was assailed by a terrible sense of bitterness. She

picked up the hair comb and brushed with hard strokes.

"I will not marry and I will never touch a man!"

* * *

"Mother, I am not interested in men. I would rather travel the world, see new places, and meet new people."

"Are you trying to hurt me?" her mother asked with a sad shake of her head, her hands firmly placed on her slender hips. Adela MacAye Roberts was a woman of serene beauty. With brown hair and deep soulful eyes, she was gifted with grace and compassion. Except when it came to Gavenia finding her *chosen one*.

"Gavenia, you have an easy life of acceptance. Do you realize how hard it can be outside the safety of Gleich Castle?"

Gavenia rolled her eyes. *Here we go again.* "Aye, Mother. I know you had a trying life as a Celtic Witch."

"*Trying* does not adequately describe the constant terror of being discovered and then burned like your grandmother."

"I am sorry for Grandma's death, but that does not mean I must be forced into choosing a husband and spending my life behind these walls."

"Not just any husband, he must be the *chosen one*."

"A man with a pure heart who calls to you … I know the proverb, Mother."

"Only he would have the bloodline that would bring healthy girls into this world to hold the ancient powers." Adela shifted a stray hair from Gavenia's face, and her voice softened. "I cannot cast the spell, only you can."

Gavenia stepped away from her mother and averted her eyes. "I will not, Mother. Can you not accept that I do not like men?"

"You need not be afraid of them, my dear. The chosen one will not hurt you."

Shaking her head, she groaned, "I do not want a

husband. Why can Callum not be the one to pass on the powers? No doubt his betrothed will be a strong lass, surely their heirs would produce another Celtic witch."

"I love your brother, but I cannot rely on his blood to sustain our powers. You know he has yet to show any signs of Celtic influence. The true magick resides in women and each generation holds an extra gift."

Her mother's eyes watered, "If I could have had more babies then I wouldn't need to burden you ... but alas ..."

Gavenia turned, and placed her arms around her mother's slim shoulders.

"'Tis not your fault, Mother. The fates have chosen for you to only have two children."

Adela smiled through moist eyes. "And I bless Arianrhod Goddess every day for you both." She touched Gavenia's face. "Perchance, I might still have another baby. Your father and I do not lack for encouragement."

"Oh, Mother!" Gavenia pushed away. "I wish not to be aware of those things."

The tinkle of her mother's giggle washed over Gavenia and she smiled in return. In times like these Gavenia saw her mother still held the presence of youth. "One day you will find a man that will make your blood heat with a mere glance and when you do, your life will be charged with a magick that goes beyond your powers."

"I do not think that will happen, Mother."

A mischievous glint shone in Adela's eyes. She grasped both Gavenia's hands and took a deep breath. Closing her eyes, she chanted beneath her breath.

"Mother, what are you doing?"

She continued to chant.

Gavenia squirmed. She did not want magick conjuring the chosen one into her life. She was not ready to die.

"Mother, you need not do this."

"Shh." Adela chanted again and then stopped, the air

crackled with energy as a blue, round light floated down from the rafters in between the two women.

"Show me a sign of who will win my daughter's heart."

"Mother!"

The orb stretched into a shield of the Robert's clan. The honorable wolf glowed bright and strong.

Gavenia said, "You see, it is of our clan. This is a sign I will not marry."

The image changed and Gavenia felt her heart beat increase. A black shadow snaked around the shield, transforming the noble crest to a demonic boar. Malevolent eyes glowed while sharp teeth dripped with dark red blood. The shadow exploded, forcing the witches apart.

Fear gripped Gavenia, twisting her insides. She glanced at her mother, whose panicked face reflected her own.

Adela gathered Gavenia into her arms. "I will not let anything hurt you."

"Dark forces surround the chosen one. How could I summon him now when he would bring death to our clan?"

"We do not know that."

Gavenia pulled away from the warm embrace. "Mother, do not act innocent. You and I both felt the power of evil."

"Perhaps the chosen one needs help."

"I would not help a stranger if it meant the clan is in peril."

"The chosen one is no stranger, he is your family. The one destined to bring you love and happiness."

"I will not do it."

"You must summon him. You must produce an heir at any cost. The future of good magick is at stake."

Tears wet Gavenia's face, unable to hold the raw emotion inside, she cried, "I cannot." Running out the door, she ignored her mother's concerned voice that called after her.

* * *

"Tell me, who am I," Tremayne slammed the heavy door behind his voluptuous sex maid and she jumped from the noise. Wringing her hands she walked further into his chamber, no doubt to put distance between his anger and herself.

Coira MacKinnon maybe a scheming, lying whore, but she knew when to retreat.

She pivoted toward him, her auburn hair tumbling around her shoulders as her hazel eyes lowered. "You are Laird Tremayne Campbell, chieftain of the clan, son to Lady Torella and the great dark sorcerer of this castle."

"I am glad you remembered, Coira." Tremayne went to his chest beneath the tall window and opened the timber lid. Without looking at her, he continued, "So tell me why you disobeyed my command?"

"Master, I wish not to leave you," she pleaded and ran to his side. She went to place her hand on his shoulder, but in the last moment, retreated. "I pray you. Send one of the old crones in my stead."

He straightened and pulled out a long whip. "Mayhap, your loyalties need to be prompted as to who is your laird."

Coira blinked, her lips curving into a smile of anticipation as she stared at the whip in his hand. "How may I assist you?" She began to unlace her ruby corset and threw it to the side, eagerness shining in her eyes.

"I know you like the whip, Coira. But this time I will *not* use it on you until you plead for forgiveness."

"Please do not tease me, Master." She lifted a calico chemise over her head; her pert breasts jutted proudly, the peaks hard and erect. Tremayne felt his member rise, throbbing beneath his kilt.

His hands cupped her breasts and she groaned. Curly,

copper hair cascaded over soft shoulders while Coira arched her back, pushing her chest forward.

"I would do anything for you my laird. I beg you to forgive my impertinence."

Taller than the average man, Tremayne looked down his nose at the contrite maid. "You will offer your services to Lady Gavenia of the Roberts clan."

Coira raised her head and scrunched her nose. "I could be of more use to you in your bedchamber my laird. Do not punish me by sending me away."

Tremayne chuckled nastily, and distanced himself from the sex maid, releasing the sexual energy he wrapped around his lovers.

Eerie, cool air surrounded his sex maid. Smiling, he watched bumps on her delicate skin. Contact with him brought women to submission, but taking that contact away sent them into a state of uncontrollable wanting. A deadly thirst for something only he could quench.

Turning, Tremayne looped the whip around his neck and walked over to the wooden table to pour a chalice of red wine. "I grow weary of your whining." Taking a sip of the tart liquid, he studied Coira's voluptuous curves. Her body had given him much pleasure, and the sexual energy he needed for his powers to increase. But he grew restless for something, and he knew not what.

"Perhaps it is time to send you back to your father. I know he could use your help in the fields," he offered.

"Nae, my laird."

She ran toward him and then halted, with sense enough to know if she touched him now, she would regret it. She backed away and lowered her head. Tremayne pursed his lips at her wisdom. She knew he did not like to be touched unless instructed to do so.

The light surrounding Coira's aura was dark red, impatient to feel the sting of his whip. Some women liked to be caressed with a tender hand while others, like his sex maid, were stimulated by power and violence. Either way, Tremayne absorbed their energy when they climaxed.

Replacing the goblet, he slowly pulled the whip from his shoulders and cracked the leather bind near her feet. The sharp sound made her body jolt, and the energy surrounding her increased with sexual tension.

"You will report to me on everything Lady Roberts does."

Coira nodded, her eyes glazed with lust and submission. Grabbing the back of her neck he turned her toward the bed and threw her face down, her bare backside exposed to him.

With a flick of his wrist the whip lightly snaked across her flesh and she groaned.

"Who her companions are."

The whip cracked in the air.

"And where she rides."

This time, the thin leather cut lightly into her flesh.

"Oh," she moaned. "Aye, it will be done. Please punish me again."

Tremayne smiled, the scent of her arousal reached him and he breathed with satisfaction. There was nothing more intoxicating than a woman's nectar. He ran the handle of the whip up the length of her inner thighs until he reached the apex.

"Spread your legs further apart," he commanded, his tone brooked no argument.

She complied and he rubbed the handle up and down her slick wet lips. A muffled sound came from the bedcovers while she wiggled against the whip.

His cock pulsed against the rough fabric of his kilt, but he ignored the constrained ache. Tilting the handle, he slowly eased it inside the sex maid. Backwards and forwards, he watched Coira's aura change from red to purple, her arousal increasing. Soon, very soon, she would give him his life force.

He increased the speed of his wrist.

"Take my whip. Take it!"

"Aye," she screamed, her body enveloping the handle further inside. She shrieked and came with an explosion, her body shuddering with pleasure. Sizzling energy gathered around her like a glowing cloak. The purple light crackled as it filled Tremayne's body, creating a mystical sensation beyond any physical pleasure. He quickly pulled out the handle and kneeled behind her. Biting his lip with frustration, he lifted his kilt and drove into her warm, pulsating core.

Thoughts of the Celtic witch fueled his anger and lust. Harder and harder he pushed inside Coira, punishing his sex maid in the witch's stead.

But it was not enough.

Soon, very soon he would be in a position to spill the blood of Lady Gavenia Roberts.

ABOUT THE AUTHOR

Photograph by Rod Vella. www.RStudios.com.au

Born in Queensland, Australia, Lyn Armstrong has a passion for writing historical romance with an erotic element. This self-confessed romantic wrote her first novel in the early 1990's and has been writing ever since. Along with touring the countries she writes about, Lyn has served on the board of Florida Romance Writers. When she is not lost in the mystical world of Scottish lairds and enticing witches, she enjoys spending time with family and friends.

Also available from Resplendence Publishing:

The Curse: Book One in the Legend of Blackbeard's Chalice by Maddie James.

"I felt as if I lived every thrilling moment of THE CURSE. Maddie James writes pulse-pounding suspense and riveting romance!"

Teresa Medeiros
New York Times Bestselling Author

Jack Porter is in hot pursuit of his kidnapped wife. Not an easy feat considering it is 1718 and the kidnapper is the notorious pirate, Edward Teach aka. Blackbeard. Determined to rescue his wife, Hannah, and take the pirate's head in the process, Jack sneaks aboard the pirate's ship but is too late. Hannah dies in his arms.

Nearly 300 years later, Claire Winslow vacations on a secluded east coast island, where the image of a man walking the misty shore haunts her. Then he comes to her one night, kisses her, and disappears. The next night they make love and he tells her his name is Jack. But did they really make love? Or was it a dream? And why did he call her Hannah?

The Curse sends Jack and Claire on a wild search through time for a powerful historical artifact – the silver-plated chalice made from Blackbeard's skull. This chalice holds the key to their destiny and their love. Only with the chalice will they be able to reverse Blackbeard's Curse.

Will they find it in time? Or are they destined to be parted by fate once more?

$6.50 e-book, $19.99 print

Rules of Darkness by Tia Fanning

One special gift...Twelve rules to follow...There are some rules that should never be broken.

They tell me that I am special, that my ability to heal mental illness is a "gift" that should be treasured and appreciated. As far as I'm concerned, I'm not gifted...I'm cursed. Nothing in this life is free, not even gifts. There is always a price to be paid somewhere, somehow.

My healing gift came with twelve Rules of Darkness, rules that I must follow at all times, until the day I die. The rules are ingrained in who I am. They dictate how I live my life when I am awake, and they haunt me when I'm asleep. *Don't look into a graveyard, Katia. Don't touch the dead, Katia. Never seek out the lost, Katia...*It's enough to drive a person mad.

And perhaps that's where I find myself now. A victim of a disease I can cure in others, but not in myself. It's madness to break the rules, and yet, I don't care anymore. I'm tired of living my life this way. I'm tired of the rules. I won't do it any more, and if that means I suffer the consequences, then so be it.

$4.50 e-book, $11.99 print

The Pirate Wench by Melinda Barron:

Can a staid, by-the-book journalist find love with a modern day pirate?

Melani Canton is about to find out. When she travels to Florida to be maid-of-honor at her best friend's wedding, she takes on an extra duty: taking a good look at *Ahoy, Matey*, the pirate- themed park where the wedding is set to take place, and writing a story that will attract visitors. While there, she meets handsome swashbuckler, Royce McKenna. Royce is a former lawyer who has given up the courtroom for life on the high seas, amusement park style.

McKenna is the co-owner of *Ahoy, Matey*. When Royce sees Melani he knows that he has to have her. Melani is not, however, the type to sleep with a man she has just met.

So Royce does what any good pirate would do. He "abducts" Melani and gives her a wild night of passion on his pirate ship, where Melani discovers that being Royce's pirate wench isn't such a bad thing. But when the time comes for her to go back to her stoic life, will Royce let her sail off into the sunset? Or will he find a way to keep his Pirate Wench?

$4.50 e-book, $12.99 print

Find Resplendence Titles at the following retailers:

Resplendence Publishing:

www.resplendencepublishing.com

Amazon.com:

www.amazon.com

Target.com:

www.target.com

Fictionwise:

www.fictionwise.com

Mobipocket:

www.mobipocket.com